"Next year's market outlook?" Jamie asked coolly. Her words were a gauntlet, a threat...a turn-on.

She kept her poker face steady, but Andrew knew her light blue eyes were saying something entirely different. *So this was a game to her?*

His smile turned predatory. "Slow in the first quarter, but gaining speed in the second and third, then a slight downturn in the fourth."

She licked her lips, and he followed the provocative movement with his eyes.

"Nope. First quarter is fast out of the gate..." she murmured, one flirtatious thumb absently caressing her throat, a slow up-and-down motion that his whole body noted with avid attention.

God in heaven.

She was seducing him.

Blaze™

Dear Reader,

I've always had a guilty fascination for money and the people who have it.

Recent profiles on self-made multimillionaires report that many of these men take their lunch to work, get $5 haircuts and drive a midsize sedan. This dichotomy just fascinated me to no end. That is, the idea of a person with huge amounts of wealth who still believes a penny saved is a penny earned. And thus our hero Andrew Brooks came into being.

Yet, as an author, it is my job to make our hero's world a living hell...er, so to speak. Therefore, I gave him a family that is an endless source of grief *and* love, and a woman who stretched his control as it's never been tested before. He's completely met his match in heroine Paige McNamara.

So kick off your shoes and dive right into the first book of THE RED CHOO DIARIES! Watch for the second book, *Beyond Daring,* in March 2007, and for the finale, *Beyond Seduction,* in May 2007 from Harlequin Blaze.

Happy reading,

Kathleen O'Reilly

BEYOND BREATHLESS
Kathleen O'Reilly

TORONTO • NEW YORK • LONDON
AMSTERDAM • PARIS • SYDNEY • HAMBURG
STOCKHOLM • ATHENS • TOKYO • MILAN • MADRID
PRAGUE • WARSAW • BUDAPEST • AUCKLAND

ISBN-13: 978-0-373-79301-3
ISBN-10:   0-373-79301-4

BEYOND BREATHLESS

www.eHarlequin.com

Printed in U.S.A.

ABOUT THE AUTHOR

Kathleen O'Reilly is an award-winning author of several romance novels, pursuing her lifelong goal of sleeping late, creating a panty-hose-free work environment and entertaining readers all over the world. She lives in New York with her husband, two children and one rabbit. She loves to hear from her readers at either www.kathleenoreilly.com or by mail at P.O. Box 312, Nyack, NY 10960.

Books by Kathleen O'Reilly

HARLEQUIN BLAZE
967—PILLOW TALK
971—IT SHOULD HAPPEN TO YOU
975—BREAKFAST AT BETHANY'S
979—THE LONGEST NIGHT

To my Dad, always frugal, never cheap

1

JAMIE MCNAMARA STOOD on the street outside Grand Central Station and shook her head in disbelief. Two million commuters were sharing the same miserable situation. Stranded, stuck, marooned in Manhattan.

Why today? Of all days. Why not tomorrow, when Connecticut really didn't matter?

"It's not an insurmountable problem," said a deep, ear-tickling voice behind her, obviously not privy to the rage that was precariously close to boiling over inside her.

Insurmountable. Yeah, right. Like she could just walk the ninety-five miles from Grand Central to Stamford—in Jimmy Choo heels, no less. Not in this lifetime.

Jamie whirled around, partially to condemn the smug voice, but there were parts of her—devious, womanly parts, that wanted to see if the face matched the vocal chords.

"Thank you for that bit of blind optimism," she said, caught by the serious, dark eyes. Almost black. Then she noticed the suit, the leather briefcase, the same gray jacket that had nearly run over her earlier as she'd dashed for what was the last running train.

Very hot, but very rude.

Just her luck. People talked about the luck of the Irish, but you never heard about the luck of the Scottish. That's because they didn't have any.

The dark eyes flickered over her again. Efficiently, like an accountant jumping right to the bottom line. Jamie felt a slight flush and then mentally flogged herself for the lapse in confidence. She was classically tailored, buffed and polished herself. "Study hard," her mom used to tell her. "There're women who coast by on their looks. We're not them."

"Excuse me," Jamie said, brushing past the tightly muscled frame. The suit didn't hide his physique; it magnified it, as only a good custom job can do.

Italian wool, too. Probably Sergei Brand. Then she realized what she was doing and stopped, reminding herself she was currently in a man-free phase, which sounded much more acceptable than "my last boyfriend married my secretary, Amber."

Todd had whined continuously about her work hours, but not to Jamie. Oh no, he spent his quality time on the phone with Amber. She'd ask him "What's wrong?"

"Nothing," he'd said. Jamie read the engagement announcement in the *New York Times* before he had the guts to tell her in person. That'd been nearly two years ago and she'd restricted her relationships to mostly non-existent since then.

The old anger erupted inside her, flowing through her like hot liquid goo. Jamie elbowed the suit's briefcase, not quite an accident, and jumped right into the Forty-second street traffic, fighting all the other commuters for the six cabs that were currently on duty. She raised her hailing hand, stepping in front of a mousy touristy type.

"We should split a car," the suit said, stepping into traffic with her.

Jamie's hand lowered. A cabbie—occupied, of course—honked for her to move, and she jumped back to the curb, before taking another long look at the suit.

Split a car?

It was a fascinating suggestion because it couldn't be economic reasons that prompted the invitation. Clearly she and he shared the same financial echelon. It could be practicality, two strangers needing to find a way out of the city when a power outage stopped mass transit.

But what if the reasons were more carnal? Good, old-fashioned lust.

Thoughts of lust during business hours wasn't Jamie's standard operating procedure; business was her ruling passion, but she felt the dizzy pull of—him.

It was rash, it was spontaneous. It was thrilling.

Briskly—because she'd already had three cups of coffee—she gave him an efficient once-over, starting at the spit-polished wingtips, then over long, long legs, up past lean hips, beyond the ogle-inducing broad chest and shoulders, taking note of the tiny dimple in the left side of his mouth, before finally coming to stare into those dark, velvety eyes.

Just her luck, the one time she felt a spark, the dark eyes were distinctly sparkless. Instead they just looked puzzled.

Jamie dismissed the moment of fantasy and sighed. "Where are you going?" she asked.

"New Haven. You?"

"Stamford."

"It would make sense," he said with a curt nod.

He seemed polite, logical, with that extra quotient of testosterone that fluttered her insides.

Jamie didn't need fluttered insides today, or any day, so she started to tell him no.

But those eyes.

Intense, sexy, and slightly geeky. Those eyes currently held her tongue in check.

You need to get to Connecticut. He's right.

Weak, very weak, McNamara.

Her insides fluttered again, she nodded. "Okay." She held out her hand. "I'm Jamie. Pleased to make your acquaintance."

"Andrew," he said. His hand touched hers briefly. Nothing too personal. The handshake was crisp, businesslike.

Andrew. The name fit. Strong, intelligent, steadfast.

He spoke again, and embarrassingly, it took her ten seconds to realize he wasn't speaking to her. He was speaking into the wireless earpiece hanging low next to his mouth.

It was a nice mouth, if you were a woman who noticed the male mouth. Jamie usually didn't, but this bottom lip belonged to a man who would never spout poetry or renegotiate a deal. Firm, decisive, driven.

Just like her.

For a moment, Jamie let herself relax. Her mother had always said she was too driven, that she'd have a heart attack before she was thirty-five. Maybe, but at least Jamie would know that she had tried. She had plans, goals, ambitions, and she could get there, heart attacks notwithstanding.

In Manhattan, you had to be hard, driven, and relentless in order to make it.

And sometimes, you needed a reward.

Jamie fished in the briefcase, finding the inside pocket that held her secret stash. She broke off the tiniest of pieces, just a bite, just a hint, just a taste, and popped it in her mouth while no one was looking.

The milk chocolate sugar rush washed over her, and she closed her eyes in bliss.

Oh, God, that was good.

Immediately the cravings struck again, but some of her mother's lectures were too deeply ingrained, so with a look of longing, she closed her briefcase, and put it away.

But *tomorrow* was another day.

They waited on the crowded sidewalk, frustrated commuters surrounding them, until finally Andrew tugged at her arm. She followed him to the south end of the block, past an interminable line of occupied cabs, hurrying pedestrians, and honking cars.

Eventually he stopped at a car and her mouth gaped.

Car was a euphemistic term only.

This monstrosity was a white Hummer limo that was as close to tacky as a black velvet Elvis.

The big chrome wheels trimmed in gold, the endless line of doors, the tinted windows—it screamed of junior proms or drunken women flinging their bras out of the roof.

Oh, God, he was in the music business.

A neat little man emerged from the driver's seat and then opened the passenger door. "Continental Cars, at your service."

"This?" Andrew asked, and Jamie was relieved to hear horror in his voice.

"It's all we have, sir. Cars are in big demand now since the trains aren't running."

Jamie averted her gaze from the vehicle, the block-long engineering defect making her corneas burn.

"Maybe a Town Car?" Andrew asked the driver hopefully.

He shook his head. "We're fresh out. Take it or leave it."

Andrew looked at Jamie, a question in his eyes.

She wanted to flee, alligator-trimmed heels poised in a northward position, but instead she weighed her options, her sensible side telling her to call Newhouse and reschedule.

Newhouse.

Now there was a name to pull her right into a Hummer.

It'd taken her three months, fourteen phone calls,

and three Powerpoint presentations to get one heel in the Newhouse door.

A lesser woman would have abandoned the situation, put a minus in the credit column and walked away, but the prize kept her in the game. Newhouse was one of the few software companies to not just survive, but thrive during the tech bust, and now they were rolling in cash. Cash that needed to be strategically invested because the bread crumbs that their current firm was earning for them were pitiful. Bond-Worthington could change all that, and Jamie, the top client-relations rep at the firm, was the one assigned to recruit them. To date, it had been an uphill battle. But Jamie was made of tough stuff.

The name Jamie McNamara meant nothing to Newhouse and his Gorgon of a secretary, but they would soon learn...

Assuming she could get to Connecticut before lunch.

She took another look at the vehicle and tried not to shudder.

Hummer limos were for sleazy account managers, girls gone bonkers, and South Beach.

She didn't like this ostentatious hulk of metal on wheels, but the Newhouse account was calling. If she had to ride in a Hummer limo, well, suck it up McNamara, there are worse things in life.

She took a deep breath and nodded, echoes of a porno soundtrack spinning in her head.

Andrew held open the door, and before she could change her mind, Jamie climbed inside.

ANDREW BROOKS HAD a conference call in ten minutes and idle conversation wasn't his forte, but thankfully, the woman didn't seem to expect him to talk. Instead, she pulled out a copy of the *Wall Street Journal* and began to read.

He nearly smiled, because he knew just how she felt. People got in the way of productivity. Always wanting to ask him advice, or talk about a hot date, or worse yet, analyze *Survivor. Survivor: The Wall Street Edition,* that's what they needed. That was one game that Andrew would win. Every time.

The limo was hideous, red leather seats and the ceiling was covered with sparkling lights that blinked on and off. He thought there was a pattern, but was afraid to discover what it was.

He glanced over at "Jamie," wondering what her story was. She was tall and sleek, clad in a dark suit that was almost masculine in its severity. But those black shoes…

He had an odd compulsion to talk to her, find out where she worked, what she did, what corporate prize resided in Stamford.

He pushed back the purple curtain over the window, saw the endless line of gridlocked cars, and sighed. Not a good day for heading to Connecticut.

Not a good day for heading anywhere.

Their lead insurance analyst in New Haven had scheduled a lunch meeting to discuss the impact of the flattening bond market. A two-second phone call could have rescheduled the whole business, but then he had bumped into the sleek dark suit, the curvaceous body, and the stiff blue eyes, and he couldn't resist. His brother would have leered, his sister would have cheered.

Andrew was just intrigued.

So what was it in Connecticut? He didn't think she was meeting a boyfriend or a lover. Ten in the morning was too early for social obligations and there wasn't any softness about her, any excitement in her eyes. And although he wasn't big on fashion, he didn't think that women wore pinstripes on a date.

"Job interview?" he asked, because she seemed nervous, her eyes straying every now and then to her briefcase.

She peered at him over the financial page. "Excuse me?"

"In Stamford," he said. "Do you have a job interview there?"

She shook the newspaper page to straighten it out. "No," she answered, and then continued reading, dismissing him.

He checked his watch. Another six minutes until his call. "Business meeting?" he asked, trying again.

This time she lowered the paper. "Yes," she answered, just as the limo jerked to a halt.

Andrew thumped against the back of his seat.

"Sorry, sir," said a voice over the loud speaker. "The Triboro is backed up tight. Want me to try the Deegan?"

There were cars stretched out over the bridge and beyond. Nothing was moving. Not the air, not the brake lights. Andrew pressed the speaker button to talk. "An accident?"

"No," said the voice. "Just the entire city thinking a power outage is a great way to gain a four-day weekend."

Jamie leaned forward, and he caught a whiff of perfume. "Can't he go faster?" she whispered.

Andrew pressed the talk button again. "Do whatever's fastest," he said, knowing in his gut that he could've flown to Connecticut and back in the time it was going to take them to travel forty-five miles. He didn't have the heart to tell her, though. She looked like she could chew nails, but no way was that getting them across the bridge.

"Whatever you say, sir. If I hear any updates, I'll let you know."

The voice cut out, leaving Andrew and Jamie alone.

"Do you think I can be in New Haven in an hour?" she asked.

"Truth or lie?"

"Lie," she said without hesitation.

"Sure. Without a doubt."

He watched as she reached a hand around, kneading the tendons at the back of her neck. Her arm lifted her breasts under the fitted suit jacket, and his eyes flickered down. Only for a minute. But she caught him and lowered her arm.

"I have a call," he said briskly, exorcising the lust from his mind. "Do you mind?"

She looked relieved. "No, go ahead. Do what you need to."

It wasn't meant as an invitation, but the image of her, skirts up, flashed in his head. A subliminal message that came and went. Andrew frowned, and spoke into the telephone headset, commanding the phone to dial the Chicago office. He'd always been a little claustrophobic, and, trapped in the car, even if it was forty feet long, was messing with his head.

He began to speak, trying not to look her way. She took her own cell out of her briefcase and dialed, holding it up to her ear.

She wasn't overtly pretty, no argument there, but there was something so controlled inside her, a pressurized spring, tightly wound. Andrew's brother and baby sister always said he was too tightly wound. That he needed to relax and get a life. One way to relax would be to pry apart those tightly wound thighs and bury himself inside her.

"Andrew?"

He jerked back into the conversation. "Repeat that, please?"

And so the boring meeting went on. He had a life. A successful, fulfilling, organized life. But it was another kind of fulfillment, sexual fulfillment, or lack thereof, that was currently tenting his pants. He took a pad of paper from his briefcase and laid it strategically across his lap.

Just in case she noticed.

She hung up on her call, putting her cell away, and pulled out a notepad of her own.

Tinny voices buzzed his ear, the words making less and less sense.

All he could think about was the one white pearl button that was three inches below her throat. Such a small, sensible button.

Andrew had the oddest desire to take the white pearl button between his teeth and pull. Just like Everest— because it was there.

THE CAR WAS STARTING to heat up. Not from the warmth in the air, but the tension. He was having a normal, mundane conversation that Jamie had heard many times before. An assortment of numbers, buzz words, and run-on sentences that permeated corporate buildings across America, yet every time she heard that voice, it was like a shot of tequila straight to the brain. The car was going to her head. Jamie didn't even like tequila.

She tried to concentrate on the paper in front of her, but his eyes were feasting on her throat, making him impossible to ignore. After a futile struggle to remain calm, she finally put the notebook away. She crossed her legs, uncrossed her legs, before settling herself with both feet planted firmly on the floor.

There was no reason to be nervous. She'd graduated Summa Cum Laude with all of three dates. She scared men off, mainly because take no prisoners ran in her family. A genetic trait that appeared when an army general mated with a dentist.

But this one…

Andrew.

There was something about him that called to her.

Something besides the immaculate Italian wool suit. Something, well…earthy.

It was new and exciting, and to be fair, new and exciting didn't happen to Jamie very often. Nothing happened to Jamie very often, which was probably her own fault, but this feeling inside her, this tiny bubble of passion, was better than chocolate.

Much better than chocolate.

Her hand moved to her throat, and his gaze sharpened.

With one tiny flutter of her hand, his eyes had narrowed, and she heard the quiet, indrawn breath. A primitive thrill pumped through her system, a feeling usually reserved for corporate IPOs and the year-end bonus. Quickly, her hand dropped to her lap.

Just as quickly, the hunger faded from his eyes, and she watched as he scribbled efficient notes on the yellow lined legal pad in front of him.

She crossed her legs, trapping a thrill between her thighs.

A moment gained, a moment lost.

Her fingers drummed impatiently on her tightly crossed legs and his gaze locked on her hand. Realizing what she was doing, she stopped.

The tension in his face relaxed and he shot her a smile of gratitude.

And he had lots of reasons for gratitude. He hadn't been chewed out by Newhouse's warden of a secretary, only moments ago, saying that "A cut power line is no excuse for tardiness."

Being a woman in the financial industry wasn't

easy. A lot of men either wanted her to be a secretary or a willing vassal for their penis, never an equal.

A man like Andrew wouldn't need to prepare like she had for one of the most ambitious deals in the history of Bond-Worthington Financial. No, he had looked happy as a clam while chatting away about margins and puts. Probably because he had a blond secretary with plasticized implants. Probably named *Amber.*

A tiny sigh escaped from her lips.

He was attractive, he was successful, *he* was a man, she reminded herself, even though parts of her were already tantalizingly aware of that fact. But what did that matter? Because of today, she was probably going to lose her deal, and she never lost a deal. She would face the walk of shame back at the office, having to explain to Walter why she couldn't leap over tall buildings in a single bound, why she couldn't start an electrical-powered locomotive, and God only knows that she couldn't stop bullets with her chest, much less traffic.

But Jamie liked being the star performer in the office. More importantly, she couldn't live without it.

It was all she had.

No, life was definitely unfair. Her eyes looked at his. Deliberately, her hand rose to her throat.

Tossing caution to the wind, she unfastened the tiny button. It was a small, insignificant gesture, nothing overt or slutty, but for one slow second in time, she wanted to disrupt his manly existence, to explore this new feeling inside her, and right some of the injustices in the world.

He stopped talking.
Blinked twice.
Swallowed.
Mission accomplished.

2

IT WAS A SMALL HALF-INCH of flesh. Not golden tan, more like pale peach. Andrew valiantly attempted to keep up with the back and forth of the conference call, but failed. Instead he was mesmerized by the lure of naked skin.

It wasn't cleavage or thigh. It was nothing but an uncovered throat.

God, he was losing it.

He dragged his eyes away from the sight of temptation and studied the lined paper in his lap, but the words blurred together. The voices in his ear buzzed like a mosquito on a summer's day and he struggled to make out the words: *"a marketing strategy to focus on old-fashioned honesty in our financial dealings."*

Okay, that made sense.

"Dave, do you think traders will really buy into that?" he asked, rather proud of himself for coming up with a halfway lucid contribution.

Even better, he could ignore her. He could ignore the raging hard-on that had blood streaming down from his brain to his cock. He could ignore the fact that he hadn't gotten laid in eight months.

Okay, that one he couldn't ignore.

It explained much of his current situation.

He'd never been a New York playboy like his younger brother, Jeff, who chased after supermodels and party girls. Most of the women who Andrew dated were classy, but not clingy. Never clingy. The idiosyncrasies of a relationship took too much time, so by default the ones who lasted were the ones who made few demands.

Whatever worked.

His gaze traveled upward, leaving the relative security of the legal pad to skim over nicely turned breasts, past the lurid throat, and finally coming to rest on her face.

Jamie of No Last Name looked to be hell on wheels. A woman who threw you down on the bed, and…

No, no, no…

He'd seen guys in the office succumb to the lure of the velvet power of the p-whip, but not Andrew. Too many people were counting on him.

That thought helped gird the loins that were currently raging with lust.

But she was cute, although he suspected she'd kill him if he said it aloud. Certainly not cute in a kitten and babies sense—thankfully. Her brown hair was pulled back in an elegant ponytail, her light blue eyes were never still, blinking to one side then another…

…blinking mindlessly while he was pounding inside her.

The loins came ungirded.

Damn.

"Drew, do you have anything to add?" asked the voice in his ear.

He cleared his throat. "No, I think we've covered it. Thanks, everyone, for dialing in. It's been a productive meeting."

It was all bullshit, and Andrew didn't usually go for bullshit, but there was a time and place for it, and when you're currently having Technicolor fantasies about the woman sitting across from you in a tank of a limo—well, bullshit didn't seem out of the question.

He snapped his briefcase closed with a bang that seemed obscenely loud. She looked up at him, and he saw a quick flash of panic. *Somebody else was nervous, too.*

Andrew stared out the window, away from the cold sweat of her gaze, and watched the cars inch forward at a snail's pace.

Distraction. He needed a distraction.

He pounded on the speaker button. "Driver, how're we doing?" he asked, like he couldn't tell.

"Two hours to Connecticut. We've almost made it across the Whitestone, sir."

"Thank you," he said politely, and then heaved a breath. While he obsessed over the currently unclothed throat of the mono-monikered Jamie, the oxygen was turning thin—all at one hundred feet over sea level.

He needed to label her, use the brand like a wedge, because it was obvious that the three feet between the car seats wasn't going to do it.

Urges, when unchecked, were a dangerous thing,

leading to forgotten responsibilities, sloppily completed tasks, and poor credit scores. Andrew had deferred gratification his entire life; there were other things more important, namely food and rent.

Drew looked over at the object of his current urge, while considering extremely inappropriate behaviors. Desperate times called for desperate measures, and frankly, the state of his hard-on was about as desperate as he'd ever been.

"SoundDesign. Gross receipts last year over forty-seven billion."

"I beg your pardon?" she asked, quirking one brow.

"The speaker company," he answered in his flattest, most monotonous voice.

"Forty-seven billion?"

He nodded. "Price per earnings of nine point seven. Low. Hold recommendation."

"You're a broker, I assume," she said, eyes sparkling, one lip curling up in that cocky half smile that was going to haunt him for days.

"Sort of," he answered, omitting that he actually managed a half-billion-dollar hedge fund that he turned a neat twenty-one percent annual profit for the last five years, beating the market average three times over.

"Fascinating," she replied, the mischievous light dimming from her eyes. Definite progress.

One of Andrew's most valuable skills in the fight against ties that bind was the ability to bore a date to death when he wanted to dump 'em.

Worked every time.

"Sergei Brand," she said.

"What?" he asked.

"Your suit. Sergei Brand. Number one maker of semi-custom. Breakout sales in the late nineties when they limited their inventory to only smaller, boutique-type tailors and cut off the big department store chains altogether. Sales climbed thirty-seven percent in the first year, and then tapered off to a blazing twenty-three percent for the next three years."

Andrew's heart stopped. Cardiac arrest at the age of thirty-six. "Are you in fashion?" he asked helplessly.

"Wall Street," she told him, casually studying her nails.

Holy, Alan Greenspan.

"Oh," was all his razor-sharp wit could come up with.

Then she looked up, her face poker-steady, but the light blue eyes were saying something entirely different. "Next year's market outlook?" she asked coolly. The words were a gauntlet, a threat…a turn-on.

So this was a game to her? Two could play at that, and Andrew's smile turned predatory. "Slow in the first quarter, but gaining speed in the second, and third, and then a slight downturn in the fourth."

She licked her lips, and he followed the provocative movement with his eyes. "Nope. First quarter is fast out of the gate."

"What about the January affect?" he asked, his voice huskier than normal.

"Not a factor. Gains in the entertainment sector will outpace all others," she said, one flirtatious thumb absently caressing her throat, a slow up and down motion that his whole body was following with avid attention.

His mouth opened, a high school caliber proposition sat on his tongue. And then he remembered his age, his college degrees, his supposed maturity. "What makes you say that?"

"The American consumer is ready to play."

She was wrong, and he knew it. "Disagree," he argued.

Furiously she shook her head until one wayward lock of hair fell loose from its rigid confine. The minx was toying with him, until his instincts honed in for the kill.

"The burgeoning consumer market is too crowded," he continued. "Everywhere there's distraction. More, more, more, everything pounding at the brain like a hammer. Eventually there's steam, billowing smoke. Before the year is out it's gonna implode because a consumer can only take so much before he erupts. It's Krakatau, Vesuvius, Mt. St. Helens. Mark my words, it'll blow."

She leaned forward in her seat, one stocking-clad knee inches from his own. Her cheeks were flushed, her pupils dilated. "That same stress will force the consumer to increasingly turn to things to take their mind off economics, politics, foreign affairs, and the price of oil. They'll need to wind down, relax. TV, movies, gaming, the Net, those are the only things large enough to fill the void," she said, her gaze locked with his, and his brain flickered off. His hands itched to pull the ponytail loose. His fingers curled, aching to follow the line of her throat, finding out what lay beneath the demure suit jacket. And his cock, well, his cock didn't need an instruction manual. No, all current thinking was going on below the waist.

God in heaven, she was seducing him.

JAMIE PERCHED ON THE EDGE of her seat, waiting. She loved to debate, any excuse to argue, and Andrew was her biggest challenge yet. She felt primitive, carnal and exquisitely female.

Yeah, okay, admit it.

She was turned on.

She'd never felt this pull of animal attraction. The hard, dark eyes were no longer hard. The spark was definitely there. And that firm mouth kept luring her gaze, the pounding of her heart matching the telling pulse between her thighs. The soft cotton of her bra rubbed unbearably against her breasts. It was exhilarating, freeing…

Titillating.

All because he was indulging in a little monetary give and take. The electric shock was zooming straight to her head, among other places. She felt invincible, Xena, modern-day warrior princess, ready to turn Newhouse and his cow of a secretary into toast. With only a snap of her fingers, Jamie would have the poor man down on his knees, begging to sign on with her firm. But first things first.

There was another man she wanted down on his knees. *And she was looking right at him.*

"CAN I ASK YOU SOMETHING?" Andrew said, although he didn't know what he would ask.

"Yes," she whispered.

"Jamie…" he started.

"Yes," she said again, leaning in closer, until he could smell her. The last lingering of her perfume, the fibrous aroma of summer wool, and the hint of musky desire.

He closed his eyes, breathing her in.

"Jamie," he tried again, but then suddenly he didn't care anymore. All he cared about was touching her, exploring her. Andrew pulled her over and into his lap. He had a tremendous need to kiss that crooked mouth, and so he did.

He usually had more finesse, but his quick wits had slowed to a drugging crawl, and his body moved with a will of its own. Her lips were soft, pliable, open for him, and his tongue shot inside. She climbed closer into his lap, her hips toying with his cock, until he was ready to beg for mercy. His hand flew to the buttons on her blouse, working one, breaking two, and exposing a wonderfully proper, cotton bra.

"We shouldn't," she murmured in a voice that only egged him on, and then she sighed against his neck, pressing warm kisses there, her tongue playing in his ear.

"We should," he answered. His hand moved to the fastening on the back of her bra, and he unclasped it in one try, which was a new record for him, last made in eighth grade at PS 117, when Erica Haberman cornered him in the boy's bathroom.

He pulled the white cotton fabric to one side, exposing a pert, rosy nipple. He took it in his mouth, pulling, tasting, feasting. She moaned again, her head falling back, exposing the creamy white throat that had started it all.

His erection pulsed and strained against her. He wanted to touch flesh. He had to touch.

His hand reached down between her legs, finding a silky set of panty hose and he broke through easily, pushing one finger inside her.

She bucked on his lap, and he heard another moan. Deeper, longer. His.

Her hands clasped his shirt, first for support, and then her fingers worked to release the buttons, and she pulled it free, running her hands up and down his chest.

"I don't usually do this," she said.

He pushed her back against the long, bench seat, and slid the sensible dark skirt down her legs.

"I know," he murmured against the creamy skin of her stomach. "You have beautiful legs," he continued, not because he thought she had beautiful legs, but because he had never been so taken over by a woman before. He didn't act on urges, he was the master of steely self-restraint. However, the close confines with her were killing him. He met her eyes, expecting to see the same odd, reckless urgency, but instead he found something that could have been nerves.

Nerves.

Cold reality intruded. What the hell was he doing? Andrew stopped the skirt-sliding because they were in a Hummer limo. Relative strangers.

For God sakes, they were in the financial industry.

"I'm sorry," he said, removing his hands from her skirt, but he wasn't a complete fool. They hovered nearby—just in case.

He waited, perched like a lion guarding his prey, his breath uneven. If he had more scruples, he would have moved back to his seat, but he couldn't. Her look, half tailored, more than half mussed, entranced him. The jacket loose on her shoulders, the blouse pulled aside, exposing the firm swell of her breasts, one nipple coyly poking out, just to tempt his fingers, his mouth.

In a Hummer, for God's sake…

JAMIE COULDN'T SPEAK even if she wanted to because her heart was pumping too fast. She wasn't impulsive, she was strategic, but she'd never considered sex like this before.

Fast, furious. If he wanted her to fling her bra out of the roof, she was just turned on enough to do it. Anything to bring that taut mouth back to her breasts, anything to keep those glorious hands between her thighs.

And there he was, his dark eyes glazed with lust. For her.

In that moment, she considered the wisdom of having a one-morning stand with a man she'd just met.

But he *had* gallantly offered her a ride to Connecticut.

"Ride" being the key concept, prompted her more cautious self.

He's no Casanova, she argued back. He was either an award-winning actor, or he was as appalled by what was happening as she was. Overcome with passion, she thought with a romantic sigh. She'd never overcome Todd with passion before; their matings were planned, scheduled, and scripted. This exuberance of passion from her was new. Maybe this was a rebound response?

She studied his face. Anxious dark eyes were watching her, not forcing her into something she didn't want to do, not even coaxing her into something she didn't want to do. Damn.

Dark, crisp hair coated his chest, tempting her fingers. He tempted her. His mind was sharp as a tack, yet he was chivalrous, and okay, built.

On the other hand, he was a man. A man who belonged to that rare three percent of the gender who would never coax. Instead he would let the woman choose her own poison, relieving him of all conscience and responsibility.

God, that meant he was probably in upper management.

The scintilating thought was enough to push her one step closer to the edge.

Slut, screamed her proper side.

Delicious, said the other.

"Do you have a condom?" she asked him, preparing to forsake the whole experience if he wasn't prepared.

If he said, "yes," it would be fate, because he didn't look like a man who carried a condom in his wallet.

Anxiety pulled at her nerves while she waited for his response. Behind her back, her fingers were crossed, because deep in her heart, she wanted her sensible half to lose.

"*Uh,*" HE ANSWERED.

"That's a 'no,'" she announced with regret in her voice, raising herself on her elbows, the shirt lapels sliding closed.

Sadly he shook his head, but then he remembered something. A mere figment in the back of his mind. The night of Kevin's wedding reception.

Did he still have it?

He fished out his wallet, and snapped it open, and there he found the gold coin inscribed with "Kevin and Marlene, 6/15/2005."

He blessed his old college roommate in that moment. "A wedding souvenir."

"Fate," she murmured.

"Indubitably," he said, and ripped the top off his salvation. "You're sure?" he asked one more time because he wanted her to be.

She gave one definite nod, and that was all the encouragement he needed.

In less than two heartbeats he was inside her.

Damn.

Andrew froze, reliving the thrill of being surrounded by woman. His whole body burned with pleasure, and he took a moment just to feel. She was tight, wet, fitting him like a glove. Her eyes clouded with emotion, soft and welcoming. Then her thighs moved, tightened around him, and all the softness disappeared. This was fire, heat, the same hot flame he was feeling.

Slowly he began to move inside her, testing her depths, seeing what she liked, discovering what she loved. There was only one condom, so this was a one-time offer, and he wanted to make it last forever—or at least the two hours that it took to make it to Connecticut.

3

WHAT HAD SHE DONE?

Jamie struggled into her clothes, the post-orgasmic passion cooling to her normally level-headed nature. The hose were beyond repair, but if there was a drug store near the Newhouse building, she might have time to get new ones.

Studiously she avoided looking at Andrew, difficult to do in the confined space of the vehicle, but with a stubbornness born to a fifth-generation Scot, she managed.

He was already shrugging into his shirt, the neatly starched linen not quite so proper anymore. Secretly she admired the strong lines of his chest. He didn't look like the gym-rat type, but those pecs weren't iron-on tattoos, either.

Ever since she had set foot in this awful car, she'd been off her game. Maybe it was the car, maybe it was him, maybe it was the way he sparked her pulse, touched her skin, kissed her like a sexy, desirable female.

The last shimmers of passion were still glowing inside her, which couldn't be allowed because she had a huge presentation in… She checked her watch.

Ten minutes ago.

Jamie rubbed the back of her neck, trying to rub away the disappointment, too. It didn't work.

"I should call you," he said, and her panicked gaze collided with his.

"Please don't assume," she started, and then trailed off miserably. Somehow the situation would have been easier if the sex had been mediocre, or even better, awful. But nooo…

They had had great sex.

In a Hummer.

And what if he'd ruined her sex life forever? What if she was destined—cursed—to only enjoy cheap, tawdry sex with complete strangers?

It was a nightmare of stupendous proportion.

"You don't want me to call? You're involved, aren't you?" he said, and to her ears, he sounded relieved.

Quickly she nodded. A white lie, but lies were made to get people out of jams.

Her cell phone rang, rescuing her from further conversations or recriminations.

"McNamara here."

"I'm sorry, Ms. McNamara, but Mr. Newhouse will be unable to wait any longer for your meeting."

Her gaze shifted to her briefcase, boring through it, letting all her tensions narrow into one tight beam. She pushed away all thoughts of hunky guy and mangled hose, letting experience and twenty years of educational instruction whip her into shape.

With one hand, she pulled her hair back into the

ponytail with a single hard twist and a tight snap of the rubber band. Her ritual complete, all brain cells now back on line and fully functioning.

"Sandy, I can you call you Sandy, can't I?" She re-crossed her legs, confidence flowing back in her veins. "I don't need much time today. We can reschedule into thirty minutes rather than the previous hour. Don't let me down, Sandy. And you know what? Maybe I can repay you with dinner tonight. I bet you know all the best places, in fact—" she whipped out her online Zagats, fingers flying "—there's a fabulous little French place I'd love to try, La—"

"Finis, Ms. McNamara. Mr. Newhouse is already overbooked this afternoon and this morning's power mishap in the city has only made things even more impossible."

"Impossible, as a word, is highly overrated, Sandy. You sound stressed. Have you been to the day spa up in the Berkshires? If you'd like, I can set you up—"

"Hold, please, while I get the other line."

"Of course," purred Jamie, talking to dead air. She noticed Andrew watching her, measuring her job per-formance and her trampled pride kicked in. She flashed him a confident smile and began to speak into her cell, in low, overhearable tones.

"He is? Perfect! I think we can arrange to discuss that as well. And the new offerings, too? I'm sure he'll be very pleased. B-W believes in the highest services available."

She waited three beats.

"Of course we're available for whatever financial needs—"

"Excuse me, Ms. McNamara, were you speaking to me?"

Sandy the Gorgon had returned.

"Another call," Jamie snapped, her face heating up, refusing to look in Andrew's direction. "About that later appointment. Maybe fourish?"

"Mr. Newhouse is unavailable. I don't know how to be more direct."

Jamie pitched her voice low. "Just ten minutes after lunch. I don't need much time. And he really needs to hear what I have to—"

"Perhaps I wasn't being clear."

At that, Jamie's stomach curdled. She glanced out the window, the rolling hills of Connecticut whizzing by. Too little, too late.

"I'm only ten minutes from the office," she tried, hoping that the steno-taking Gorgon had a heart.

Sandy the heartless Gorgon hung up.

"Problem?" asked Andrew.

"Nothing I can't handle," she said with a tight smile.

"I'm sorry," he said, sensing that maybe her year had just been shot straight to hell, and thinking that one apology, accompanied by a sexy, yet insightful regard would make it all better.

What a chauvinist.

"It's certainly not your fault," she answered, although she wanted to blame him. She wanted to blame ConEd, the Metropolitan Transit Authority, and possibly the entire planet, because first and foremost, when it came to business, *Jamie never lost.*

"I could try and reschedule my lunch plans," he offered, still trying for helpful and Boy Scoutish, which only increased her anger.

"Look, I don't need your help. I don't need your assistance. I don't need your pity. I'm a Wellesley grad, you know. Summa Cum Laude," she added, because she needed to assert herself—regain her footing.

"What a surprise," he said, so innocently she was immediately suspicious.

When a Boy Scout turned snarky, it was time for a rethink. "I'm sorry. It's been an awful day," she offered, rubbing her neck, working to ease the perpetual ridges of tension.

He raised his eyebrows, his dark eyes holding something more than a spark. Now they held a memory. The squishiness in her thighs bloomed anew.

Bitchy as she felt, she wasn't completely vile. "No, that part was nice."

Slowly he bowed his head. "My vanity thanks you."

"Somehow I don't think your vanity needs it."

"Strokes are always…" He covered his eyes. "Strike that."

His discomfort struck something within her, because she felt it, too. Carnal overtones were still thick and heavy in the air, a new experience for Jamie, an experience that made her want to clutch her briefcase to her chest. It was her crutch, she knew it, she admitted it, and she wasn't going to loosen her grip.

Her fingers itched to get a bite of chocolate from her briefcase, but he would see it as a weakness, so she made a fist instead.

"Can you have the driver let me off at the train station in Stamford?"

"You're just going to sit and wait until the trains are running again? At least let him take you back to the city."

He didn't seem to understand that she had to leave this pleasure-cruise on wheels. The smell of sex, cologne and newsprint mingling together into a potent aphrodisiac was weakening her mind, and she couldn't have that. This was an experience best forgotten, or if not forgotten, then at least filed in the "Mistakes I'll never make again" folder.

"No, thanks," she said.

"If it's the cost, don't worry. I'll pick it up."

Like she was some minimum-wage slacker. "I can manage my own finances, thank you."

"Just a gesture, not a judgment on your earning potential."

"I'm sorry," she said. "I'm not usually like that." It was a lie. She usually was. Her nickname at the office wasn't Porcupine for nothing. Her coworkers didn't think she knew, but jokes spread, and one day she entered the break room one minute too early. Thinking fast on her feet, she pretended she didn't hear—pretended her cell conversation was still going on.

She'd fooled them all, but she wasn't sure she could fool Andrew. She pulled out her computer and began to work, shutting out Hummer limos, great sex, the uncomfortable dampness between her thighs, and Andrew. Well, not quite Andrew.

The quiet in the car grew to ear-blasting levels. The flick of fingers on the keyboard, the rustle of papers, and the sound of two people desperate to avoid a conversation.

Her in-box wasn't even cleared when the driver announced they'd arrived.

"So soon?" she said, a poor joke, but she wasn't feeling happy. Explaining to her boss about missing Newhouse wasn't going to be easy. Rain, sleet, snow or power outages. Nothing would deter Bond-Worthington.

Until today.

Jamie pulled out two twenties from her wallet, not enough to cover her share, but it was all the cash she had on her. "You can bill me for the rest," she told him, because she didn't like debts, not to credit card companies, not to people.

"I can take care of it…" he started, but apparently noticed the militant gleam in her eyes. "So how do I get in touch with you?" he asked, trapping her neatly.

Reluctantly, she pulled out her business card, and he tucked it away in his breast pocket. "I won't abuse it. Swear."

"You're a nice man," she started.

He held up a hand. "Not the 'nice man' speech."

"It's a compliment."

"Then why don't you want to go out?" he asked, a perfectly logical question, which told her he hadn't bought her earlier "I'm involved" lie. He'd probably thought no man could be involved with such a bitch.

And if the dog collar fits... So why did he want to see her again?

She noticed the torn stockings lying in the corner and sighed, a very visual clue why he wanted to see her again. Now seemed the time to share the cold, hard truth.

"I watch one hour of TV every day, the national news and Lou Dobbs. I'm on a first name basis with the delivery man from Golden Noodle. I rarely see the sunrise because I'm already at work, and I don't like chick-flicks."

"You watch Lou Dobbs, too?"

"I'm not who you think I am—I'm not a woman who has sex in a Hummer with a stranger. At least not normally," she muttered after a pause.

"You think that's the only reason I want to see you again?"

She chose not to answer, instead lugging her briefcase out of the car. Andrew would be a hi-def memory. Something to tuck away into the ten most memorable mistakes she'd made in her life. *In a Hummer.*

With a regretful sigh, Jamie walked away. Mistakes were not to be repeated. Ever.

LATER THAT AFTERNOON, the world righted itself. The trains ran, and Jamie returned to Lower Manhattan. The elevator ride to the thirty-eighth floor of Two World Financial Center would have been easier with a knife sticking out of her gut. With each passing floor,

Jamie's dread grew by percentages unheard of in the financial sector.

A power outage was normally a valid excuse for *dealus interruptus*, but Jamie was senior client relations manager extraordinaire, the legendary sales specialist who brought in the infamous Joe Tableone because she knew exactly what forty-year-old bottle of Scotch he coveted. Thomas Harris Winchell III had been persuaded to try out Bond-Worthington for a year, simply because she promised he'd never go back—well, that and a free bump to their Platinum level of customer service. Three years later, he was still a satisfied Bond-Worthington client. No, when it came to client relations, nobody could touch Jamie McNamara.

But today there was no joy on Wall Street, because Mighty Jamie had struck out. Okay, so she was being overly dramatic, but the truth was that she'd been somewhat confident when bragging about her ability to bag Newhouse for the firm. Modesty never got you anything, but a seat at the back of the room.

The elevator doors slid open with a discreet whoosh, and Jamie walked the sensible gray carpet, down cubicle alley to Walter's office. Her eyes stayed glued ahead, the better to ignore the knowing looks shooting in her direction.

"McNamara, how did it go?"

Jamie stopped and turned to face a cheerful intern, Sanji Dykstra. Sanji was both genuine and happy, a breed apart from the usual blood-thirsty crop of Ivy Leaguers betting their fortunes at a brokerage house.

His round, coffee-colored face and brown, guileless eyes would doom him to failure in the industry, but he had less than eighteen months to graduation, and she didn't have the heart to crush his dreams.

Jamie shot Sanji a thumbs-up. "I've got him just where I want him," she answered, and continued the long, solitary walk.

Then another head popped up from the alley. A blond, coiffed one, with hair way more manageable than the traditional McNamara do.

"What happened to your hose, Jamie?" asked Lindsey Feldenberg, another intern, not quite as guileless as Sanji.

"A cat jumped on my leg. Very weird. Probably a reaction from some chemical fumes in the area. Made it freak. Nasty business. I had to ditch the hose. Torn to bits," she ended.

"I don't see any claw marks," Lindsey said, blinking her big, blue eyes, but her voice was ice cold. "Nothing but lily-white skin."

Lindsey didn't like Jamie, and she'd made it very clear from the first day. Jamie was the competition and Lindsey thought she could outperform her. Lindsey had even told her that while calmly sipping from her coffee.

As an intern? Ha. When pigs fly.

Jamie had kept her mouth shut, but Lindsey's constant innuendo's were starting to draw blood.

"My skin is very thick. Claws don't leave marks."

Lindsey looked like she might argue, but then

realized the uselessness of that action, and sat down with a slightly muffled, "Bullshit."

Jamie smiled sweetly. *"Gesundheit."*

Walter's office loomed ahead like the dark basement in a horror film. She considered running back to her desk for the spare set of hose she kept in the bottom drawer, or possibly a sharp pencil to stab in her eye, but she'd gotten this far, and Lindsey, the eagled-eyed wonder would make a big to-do, and Walter really didn't care if she walked around in a bathrobe as long as she brought in the deals.

Helen, Walter's secretary, guarded the heavy paneled doors with a Fort Knox-like zeal. She was five years from retirement, and had been Walter's secretary since he started. With her tight gray curls and trembling mouth, she could have worked in a bakeshop, or been someone's kindly grandmother, but when crossed, Helen grew long, wicked fangs and could outglare even the nastiest nasty.

Which was why Jamie loved her.

"Afternoon, Helen. He asked for me to stop by when I got back."

"Yes, dear. He's on the phone with the auditors. Be careful. He's in a particularly foul mood today."

Damn, damn, double damn. "You told him the meeting got cancelled?" asked Jamie.

Helen nodded. "Hit him right after lunch with the bad news, just like you asked."

"Thanks for helping," Jamie answered, then took a deep breath, preparing to wrestle the lion in his den.

After a quick run-through of all possible excuses, she opened the door, entering the world of high-luxe.

The vice presidential offices at Bond-Worthington were old-school. Mahogany paneling, the requisite trophy wall littered with degrees, and padded leather chairs that both rocked and rolled. A VP at B-W wouldn't be caught dead with an art print or a family photo, or any bit of evidence to indicate you didn't eat, breath, sleep and ruminate solely for the firm. There were rules on Wall Street, and Jamie had learned early on to follow them to the tenth decimal place.

"Afternoon, Walter," she said, shooting for cheerful and confident. She seated herself in front of his desk with one tiny rock of her chair to convey the necessary arrogance.

Walter harrumphed. You could judge his emotional well-being by the way he cleared his throat. Low and guttural was bad. Clenched teeth and a tick meant the coast was clear. Today's forecast was afternoon storms. He peered out over silver-framed rims, just as a vice president of Financial Opportunities should.

"You let me down, McNamara. Failed me. I needed you to go out and hit a long ball, instead you stood at the plate while Newhouse threw you three breaking balls. Some other execs, you might have been able to stare them down, but Newhouse is one tough cookie."

"I know, Walter. I'm working to get on his calendar again."

"But when, McNamara? When?" He got up and

stood at the window, pointing to the view of the Statue of Liberty. "See that? That's New York. Priciest real estate in the continental U.S. And do you know how we can afford a view like this? Performance, performance, performance. Our team is the best, Jamie. We deliver every time we step up to the plate. Every time. You're at the plate. You need to deliver."

Jamie cleared her throat, low and guttural. "Got it, boss. The power outage—"

"Admit it. You got caught with your pants down."

She jerked forward, her conscience working overtime. How could he possibly... Then she relaxed. Of course he didn't know that it wasn't *her* fine Italian wool pants that had been down, exposing the tightest butt her hands had ever explored.

Instinctively, her hips rolled forward.

No, no, no.

"We must prepare for all contingencies," Walter continued. "Do you know how many times the power has gone down in the city? Two point three annually since 1970. Two contributing factors. Weather and construction. Look at that April sky! Not a cloud in it, but hear those jackhammers pounding away?"

Jamie nodded, mainly to humor him. On the thirty-eighth floor, they heard nothing but the occasional whistling of the wind. It wasn't time for semantics.

"Construction. Why do you think we keep a backup generator in this building? Our clients count on us; they expect us to be here day in, day out. 24/7. At

Bond-Worthington, we anticipate a market movement before it happens. *Before it happens.*"

"Yes, sir. I understand, sir." Jamie swallowed and continued to nod, trying to listen, needing to listen, but instead little scraps of memory played in her head.

Andrew.

There was such uncontrolled heat, such—wickedness in their lovemaking. She felt a giggle rise in her throat. It was like a soap opera or something. Jamie had neat, orderly sex, not wild monkey sex.

Primly she crossed her legs tighter.

But that didn't stop the tingles.

"Don't let it happen again, McNamara."

Guilty as charged.

Jamie looked up and met Walter's paternal gaze. She was his protégée, his pet, and a morning mambo in a Hummer wasn't going to do anything to advance her career. Hell, at thirty-two, she was well past the optimal dating age, well past the morning mambo age, too. No, her path was well-defined and well-trod. She wouldn't disappoint. She placed her feet firmly on the floor and stood up, ramrod straight.

"It's not going to happen again, sir."

He gave one curt nod. "Knock him dead, McNamara."

And with that, Jamie walked out, leaving all the tingles behind her.

4

SUZIE Q WAS ONE OF New York's most exclusive gentleman's clubs. The girls were legendary for their movie-star looks and machine-gun breasts, but Andrew ignored the undulating skin, instead choosing to stare into the murky gold liquid of his beer.

The day had been entirely wasted. Instead of analyzing the first quarter figures for Nikolson-Ploughing Pharmaceuticals, he'd stared at the numbers, remembering the awed expression that had flashed through Jamie's eyes as he'd moved inside her.

And after work, he'd thought he could catch up. Wrong, the memories were still there, and for the first time in longer than he could recall, the stock market wasn't so fascinating. Spending a Friday night at some bachelor party, burning a few more brain cells seemed justified. Besides, due to the lucky condom souvenir from Kevin's bachelor party, it seemed preordained. When Jeff had showed up at his door, he shrugged and went along like a happy, sated lemming.

Sated being the optimal word. This morning with Jamie was probably the pinnacle of his sexual career, a conquest to file away under the heading Top Ten Best Ever.

Damn, he'd been good.

His body twitched in appreciation.

There'd been this electric connection with Jamie. Something he hadn't felt in so long, he'd thought it was dead. She'd made him feel—primal, a masculine instrument of phallic proportions, created for the sole purpose of pleasing his mate.

Sure, Andrew was used to pleasing women, but they only saw the image—rich, single, not too shabby in the looks department. Andrew could be impotent, and women would throw themselves in his direction because the package was something they wanted.

But not Jamie.

He smiled, remembering the feel of her full breasts in his hands. Now that—

"Earth to Andrew." Jarred out of the steamy fantasy, Andrew looked up, and found his brother staring at him curiously. "There's only one thing that can put that drunken leer on your face, bro. A ten percent uptick in the market."

Jeff was three years younger than Andrew by birth, but light years off in emotional maturity. With proper guidance and a firm hand, he'd probably wise up—in another forty years.

Andrew took a long draw on his beer, mainly to shake off the remaining memories of the morning. "I can appreciate the female figure just as much as any man."

"Only if she's wearing a calculator. Wake up and

smell the cheesecake, bro. We're in the land of Bacchus & Boobs." To prove his point, Jeff pointed to the main stage where a perfectly proportioned Barbie doll was grinding against a pole, her bare breasts sliding up and down, up and down, up and—

Okay, Andrew wasn't dead.

"It's a nice place," he offered lamely.

"Are you completely insane?" Jeff signaled for the waitress. "You need to live, Andrew. You're going to die, and they won't be able to shoot embalming fluid inside you, because your blood turned to stone a long time ago."

"One of you is all this family can afford."

"Because I'm a slave to the lure of the feminine mystique? That's totally unjustified."

"Actually, if all you did was look, I wouldn't be worried. One of these days, you're going to hook up with the wrong girl and parts of you are going to start falling off."

A waitress came up to Jeff, climbing into his lap as if she belonged there, or at least could be rented for a fifteen-minute interval.

"You're ancient, Andrew," he continued without missing a step. "These are the best years of our lives, and you're throwing it all away." As Andrew watched, Jeff slipped a twenty in her G-string and the waitress stroked Jeff's cheek, her hand drifting down to his lap.

"Drinks?" she asked.

"Two shots of Jagermeister."

Alarmed, Andrew started to protest. "Oh, no."

Jeff flashed him an evil grin, as the waitress wiggled

back to her feet. "Oh, yes. In fact—" He patted one sculpted butt cheek "—make it six."

She brushed against him, a flirtatious shimmy of silicone. "Whatever you need, honey. Just call."

A mere four shots later, Andrew had developed a new appreciation for his brother's Bohemian way of life. That was the beauty of the public relations business Jeff was in—they didn't make shit, but by God, they knew how to have fun.

Jeff pointed a swaying finger in the groom-to-be's direction, some doofus in a brown shirt that Jeff had called Peter when they had first come in. Said victim was currently enjoying a lap dance from Trixie, Dixie, something "ixie."

"Andrew, how old are you?"

"Thirty-three, no, thirty-six. Definitely thirty-six."

His brother stared balefully. "And when's the last time you got laid."

Andrew didn't hesitate to reply. "Eleven-seventeen a.m. On the Connecticut turnpike."

And for once, Jeff Brooks, legendary media spin-master, had no words. Eventually his mouth closed, and Andrew's glow only increased. "I don't believe it. You can't have sex while driving. I've tried. Doesn't work."

"Can in a limo."

"A limo?"

"A Hummer," murmured Andrew, pleased that for once, his exploits could be bandied about in locker-room talk.

"Nah. I don't believe it. You've been reading *Penthouse* again, haven't you?"

Andrew crossed his heart. "Swear. We both needed to get to Connecticut, the trains were shut down. I gave her a ride."

"You didn't."

"I did."

"A Hummer?" Jeff lifted his glass. "I have sold you short all these years. Damn, bro. What else have you been holding out on?"

"Lots," lied Andrew, enjoying his moment in the spotlight.

"Who was she?"

"Can't name names," answered Andrew, though he might be drunk, he was a gentlemanly drunk.

"Model?" was Jeff's first guess, because he couldn't comprehend a woman off the runway.

"Wall Street."

Jeff just shook his head, letting a dancer slip into his lap. "Give us a kiss," he told her, and the redhead complied. When she had withdrawn her tongue from Jeff's tonsils, Jeff's fuzzy gaze returned to Andrew. "I don't believe it."

Andrew just shrugged.

"Was it good?"

"Five stars."

"Five minutes," scoffed Jeff.

"Try ninety, little brother."

The dancer looked at Andrew with new and more appreciative eyes. Andrew flashed her a grin. Let her dream.

"You are lying your ass off."

Andrew shrugged and lifted another shot glass. "Don't care if you believe me or not," he said, before sending the shooter down his throat. He put a fifty in the redhead's G-string. He'd regret it in the morning, but right now he felt like a king. "Buy yourself a drink."

She made a move to climb into his lap, but he waved her off. "Save it for the ones who really need it."

She looked a little miffed, and then walked away.

"Why did you do that?"

"I just saved you a thousand bucks, Jeff."

"Does it always have to be about money? I can take care of myself. I'm an adult."

"Only according to the laws of the great state of New York."

"You just don't want to admit we don't need you anymore."

Andrew frowned, the alcoholic haze dimming some. The fleeting panic abated as he realized his brother wasn't serious. "I paid for your rent," he said to remind his little brother about the rules of order in the family hierarchy.

"Not in the last six years."

Andrew frowned into his shotglass. "I paid for your college. Harvard. Stanford. Good places, not cheap. You could've picked a state school, but no…"

"I paid you back."

But not the interest, thought Andrew to himself.

Jeff read his mind. "I'll write you a check. What do you say, five percent interest fair? Hell, I'll give you eight," he offered quickly.

Andrew attempted to smile. "Keep it. Consider it a gift," he said, not because he was overly generous, but because he couldn't give up that last hold over his family.

"Tell me about the mystery woman."

"Not much to say."

"She's a dog?"

Andrew's head shot up. "Bite your tongue. Not flashy, but she's got something. Sexy, but in an understated way."

"Stacked?"

Andrew used his hands, thinking until he got Jamie's size right.

Jeff slapped him on the back again, and Andrew held onto the bar to keep from toppling. His head was starting to spin, the hangover already starting, and who knew what sort of trouble his brother could get them into.

"We should leave," Andrew said. "I'll have to break out the credit cards if we stay much longer."

"You, using a credit card? It's one of the Four Signs of the Apocalypse. We definitely should leave."

"Are you calling me cheap?"

"Did you send flowers to the mystery woman? Or perfume or lingerie?"

"She's not the type."

Actually, Jamie McNamara defied a type. Yeah, she was hard as nails, but when she got the "oh, shit" call, he'd watched her in action. Pushy, but not obnoxious. Resolved even after her butt had been wirelessly kicked from Connecticut to California and back. Still, she got over it. She had picked herself up, brushed herself off, and sashayed away, never missing a step.

Hell, Andrew had employees that couldn't do half that. No, she was one in a billion, and the sex had been one in a billion, too.

Maybe Jeff was on to something here.

Jeff looked at his brother through the empty shot glass. "Not the type? All women are the type."

"Not this one."

"You should at least send her something. An abacus."

Andrew frowned.

"That's a joke," his brother said.

"What would you send her?" Andrew asked, because the more he thought about it, the more he realized his brother was right.

"Lingerie. Classy, but sexy. Not slutty. Women like it when you don't think like a man. Classy is about as far as you can go and still be labeled sensitive."

"No lingerie. Bad idea."

"Chocolate. Or a spa treatment."

A spa treatment? Andrew remembered the way Jamie kept rubbing her neck. A massage wouldn't be a bad idea. His hands flexed, thinking of the bare, ivory shoulders, knotted with tension. He'd start with the neck, then work his way down…

"A professional," Jeff interrupted.

Andrew locked his hands away. "I knew that." If he gave her a gift, simply as a gesture to indicate his gratitude for…no, strike that. Gratitude was all wrong. "Thinking of you," he murmured. "I need something that says 'thinking of you.'"

Jeff shook his head. "Mistake, Andrew. I know the

female mind. It's a dangerous bear trap, jaws open wide, one wrong move and—BAM!" Jeff clapped his hands together. "You're history, never to experience sex in a Hummer again."

"Can we move past that?"

"You were the one bragging about it."

"I wasn't bragging."

"You're still the one who brought it up."

"Only to prove my point."

"You still brought it up."

Andrew rubbed his eyes. "We can't be related. It's impossible."

"Give me a break. I'm tons better than Mercedes."

Andrew latched onto the subject of their sister with relief. "Have you talked to her recently? She never returned my call from Tuesday."

"She's probably still pissed because you didn't cosign for that apartment."

"She's twenty-five, she should be able to manage her own things. Anyway, the place was a dump, way over-priced, and there's no grocery within twenty blocks."

"You checked it out?"

"Of course."

"Can't cut the cord, can you?"

Andrew got up. "Can we leave?"

"What are you going to give the Hummer Honey? Tell me and then we leave," answered Jeff, sticking to his bar stool like glue.

"Don't call her that."

"If I had a real name…"

"Hell will freeze first."

"Okay, but you need to send her something. That coupling was a monumental achievement in your life, a shining light in a love life that was previously best described as 'blah.'"

"Ass."

"Send her something."

Andrew slapped a fifty on the counter. "Let's go before I bankrupt myself. Give the victim, uh, the groom, my regards."

"Who?" asked Jeff, a confused, slightly drunk grin on his face.

"Peter? Remember?"

Jeff nodded. "Oh, yeah." He lifted a hand and waved in the general direction of everyone.

There was something rotten in this joint, and it wasn't the gin. "There never was a bachelor party, was there?"

"I lied." Jeff threw an arm around his older brother. "Just practicing a little quality family time."

"Freeloading. That's what you're doing. At two hundred bucks an hour."

"I love you, man."

Andrew rolled his eyes. "Go to hell," he said, with the very best familial overtone. But he did owe his brother something; Andrew needed to find the perfect gift for one Jamie McNamara. Unfortunately, he had no idea what that perfect gift would be.

SATURDAY MORNING, ANDREW AWOKE with a large hangover and the firm belief that someone was pounding a hammer inside his head. He rolled over, trying to bury his head in a pillow, but instead he rolled off his own couch.

Damn.

This was all his brother's fault.

If not for Jeff, he wouldn't have had God only knows how many shots, he would have made it all the way to his *bed* and gotten a perfectly marvelous night's sleep—weaving elaborate fantasies around Jamie McNamara, her long legs, tight rear, firm, gravity-defying breasts...

Okay, he probably wouldn't have gotten any sleep, but at least his head wouldn't sound like a construction site.

Cautiously, he tried to stand, but something kept pulling at him. He opened his other eye and realized that his currently still-attached tie was stuck between the couch cushions.

Jeff was really going to feel pain for this. Andrew wasn't exactly sure how, but an innocent, honorable man shouldn't have to suffer this much from alcohol.

He unknotted his tie and threw it over the nearest chair. He looked down at the wrinkled shirt and pants, but there were more important problems to address.

Namely his head.

Aspirin. That was what he needed. He took two halting steps toward the bathroom and realized the pounding wasn't coming from his brain, it was coming from outside in the hallway.

Andrew flung open the door, only to be greeted with an empty space. Then the hammering began again.

Two doors down.

A young guy stood at the door, curly-haired in torn jeans and a rocker-chain snaking out from one pocket.

The guy looked up and quickly looked away.

Andrew scowled.

From the far end of the hallway, another door opened and Estelle Feldman peered over her security chain. The octogenarian resident of 43B had occupied the place since the early sixties, or at least that's what George the doorman had told Andrew.

Old Lady Feldman glared at the door pounder at 43C, then hmmmmppphed before slamming her door closed—hard. The shot echoed inside Andrew's head.

He closed his door, wondering why everyone had to be up at seven thirty on a Saturday morning. Actually, Andrew was normally up at five thirty on a Saturday morning, and if hadn't been for all those shots…

Damn it, Jeff, he thought, applying blame where it belonged. Squarely on Jeff's shoulders.

He plodded into the bathroom, popped four aspirins, and then made some extra-strength coffee.

At some point in time, he was going to have to work.

But then he collapsed back on his couch, putting the pillow over his head, letting the aspirin work its magic. The cottony fabric was plump and reminded him of Jamie's breasts. He smiled and pulled the pillow closer.

At some point in time, he would go back to work. However, Andrew calculated that there were at least three hours of elaborate fantasies that he'd missed out on.

Right now, he intended to make up for it.

BRIGHT AND EARLY MONDAY morning, before the rest of the suits arrived, Jamie found a small package on her desk. Glimmering silver wrapping paper, trimmed with an overlay of flowers, and a red velvet bow. Elegant, but the outer covering didn't give her a clue about what was inside, who had sent it, or where it came from.

Never one to stand around and contemplate the issue, she dove right in, fingers flying. Jamie loved surprises, loved the thrill of opening presents, mainly because no one in her family was impulsive. Christmas and birthdays were about the only time when a plan wasn't created, discussed, implemented, and then followed up by the requisite postmortem critique of how they as a family could do better.

Eventually she had the box ripped down to the bland, white anonymous cardboard, and she was still no closer to figuring out what was inside. The four sides were all taped, top and bottom, too, the product of a masochistic mind, she was sure. Jamie grabbed for the scissors from the office supplies cabinet, and four snips later, she discovered that she was the proud owner of a—

Magic eight ball.

What the heck?

She turned the ball upside down to check out her fortune, not that she believed in that kind of snake oil nonsense.

"The market will move down today."

"Oil futures are up."

"Take a coffee break."

"The market will move up today."

And the next one, the most tantalizing, mysterious of all—

"Someone is thinking of you."

Andrew. He hadn't seemed like a novelty toy giver, but the choices were limited. Her exposure to human beings was small, and yeah, okay, she'd been doing a little thinking about him. Apparently he'd been thinking about her, too.

Maybe?

She shivered in her seventy degree office, just as the phone rang at her desk.

"I couldn't resist," was his opening line and she fought the juvenile urge to dance.

"You didn't have to," she answered.

"But are you glad I did?"

"Yes," she whispered.

"I'm glad you're glad," he whispered back.

She walked around the desk and kicked the door closed with her heel, wanting to keep Andrew separate from the hurly-burliness that was work.

"How was your meeting on Friday?" she asked, a girly question in a girly voice. She hated the weakness in herself, but she loved the gift. Impractical, yet calorie-free. He must've thought she was whimsical and funny. Although he was completely wrong, she loved that he thought that about her.

"The meeting was boring. A complete waste of time," he answered.

"I'm sorry."

"You should be. You're responsible."

"You're blaming me?"

"Yeah."

A secret smile curled on her lips. *She'd distracted him.* "I'm sorry."

"Sorry enough that you'll go out with me tonight? Something simple. No mass transit involved. Dinner, or if that's too much, just drinks. Coffee even."

"I'll be in D.C. tonight."

"Hate the traffic."

"What about Tuesday?"

"Can't. Going to Houston to meet with an oil company."

"Oh," Jamie answered, completely disappointed, but she knew it was for the best. She couldn't do this. She needed to keep her focus.

However, Andrew wasn't done. "What about Friday? After six, though. The CPI report is coming out at four, and I'll have some work to do."

"Me, too," she answered, one heel skimming back and forth on the carpet, the intimate tone in his voice making her forget about work.

"Say yes?" he pressed.

Her ringless fingers drummed on the mouse pad, caution signs flashing in her brain. She didn't have time for a relationship, even time for a fling. Especially now with the Newhouse account hung around her neck like a seven-figure albatross.

But would a few hours of happy-time really matter? What sort of damage could one night really do?

Jamie picked up the magic eight ball, and watched the message appear in its watery text.

Say yes.

"You've ruined me," she said aloud.

"What do you mean?" he asked cautiously.

"I was supposed to finish a report on Friday."

"Finish on Saturday."

"I needed to review the second quarter housing forecast, and then I have about ten PRER14As to go through."

"And what were you supposed to do on Sunday?"

"Sunday is my day of rest. I sleep late, wake up to the smiling face of Tim Russert, and read three days worth of the *Wall Street Journal, Business Week,* and *Forbes.*"

"No *Fortune?*"

"That's on Monday."

"You've a very busy lady, Jamie McNamara."

"Not too busy for dinner on Friday."

"That's an affirmative?"

She leaned over her computer, and typed Andrew into the appointment box. "I just put you on my calendar. You're official. Where do you want to meet?"

"I'll wait for you in the lobby of your building. Say eight o'clock?"

"It's a date," she answered, nearly a sigh.

5

THE DAY TRIP TO D.C. GAVE Jamie the shot in the arm she needed. For the past three years, Smithson-Hughes, a primary defense contractor, had been watching over their B&W portfolio like Scrooge McDuck, pinching every penny, arguing over fees, never feeling like they were getting a fair deal. In return, B&W had bent backward, sideways, longways and every which way to accommodate the eternal audits, but finally, finally, *finally,* they gave Jamie the atta-girl she'd been seeking from them—a new three-year contract and a bottle of champagne.

Feeling the love, Jamie had glanced around the conference table, noting all the four-star generals, the quintessential old boys club. These were her father's peers, and for one day at least, she was in.

The high lasted into Tuesday and she decided to do something impulsive. To do something just for her. So on her lunch hour, she went back to her apartment building, grabbing a midday workout in the gym.

The gym on the seventeenth floor was one of the reasons she loved her building. The setup was perfect, a large wooden floor with four mirrored walls. There were the usual cardio machines: treadmills, ellipticals, stationary bikes and Stairmasters, an assortment of Nautilus equipment and free weights, which Jamie didn't believe in because a day only had twenty-four hours. However, the elliptical was her friend. She had done a sweat-drenching half hour when Krystan, the gym trainer, appeared, slapping her on the back. "Excellent, Jamie. Keep workin' it. Feel the burn."

Jamie struggled to smile. "Trust me, the burn is being felt."

Sadly, Krystan was a twenty-year-old blonde who had another ten years before her body started breaking down. Jamie tried not to hate her; it was a struggle.

Krystan climbed up on the elliptical next to her and started to pump away. "So tell me how the job is going?"

This was the usual conversation starter from Krystan. She was in tune with her clients' successes and failures, and smartly refrained from asking about Jamie's social life. However, it was only four days until Friday, and this one time Jamie was dying for Krystan to ask her about her love life. "The job is going well, but I've been doing other things—going out, having a life, skipping a working lunch."

Krystan ignored the hint. "Sounds great! Ready to pump some iron? Those biceps are looking droopy!"

Appalled, Jamie looked down, because her biceps did not droop. Not one part of her drooped, nor ever would.

"Made you look," Krystan said with a laugh.

When a woman was drenched with sweat, hair bunched into a ragged ponytail, and still needed to burn an extra three hundred calories from the half chocolate bar that she'd eaten that morning, Krystan's jokes weren't really that funny. "What did you do this weekend?" she asked through gritted teeth.

Krystan laughed and cranked up the resistance on the machine. "Oh, the usual. We jogged through Central Park, and then Bryan decided to surprise me with breakfast in bed. Poached eggs with grapefruit juice. Gotta love the man," she said, ending with a sigh.

Breakfast in bed? Jamie wondered if Andrew ever made breakfast in bed. She chewed on her lip, wondering. He hadn't seemed like the overly impractical type on Friday, but then on Monday, he'd sent her a customized eight ball. Completely impractical.

Breakfast in bed, while thoughtful and considerate, was also majorly impractical.

When she was a kid, and they'd lived on the base in Florida, one morning she'd snuck a chocolate chip waffle into her bed. The whole thing had been a huge mess, and Jamie had learned about the impracticality of eating breakfast in bed.

Still…

"Breakfast in bed sounds great! We're going out this weekend. I'm not sure where yet, he's going to surprise me," Jamie said, taking Krystan's breakfast in bed and raising it one dinner surprise.

Krystan looked at her and smiled in confusion.

Oh, well. So much for the female bonding moment.

Just then the students from the class began filing again, and Krystan slowed down, hopping off the machine.

"Ladies, ladies! You're just in time! Tone those abs, tighten that ass, get those thighs rock-solid!"

After a quick wipe-down, Jamie trudged over to the mats where the class was about to begin. All good things in life came from work and self-discipline. If it didn't hurt, then chances are, it wasn't worth doing.

Pilates, for anyone who'd ever had the pleasure of not experiencing it, was a hellish exercise system invented by a man—of course. It involved contorting the body into strange poses by the use of foreign objects.

Foreign objects—innocent objects—that previously were used for play were now instruments of body torture. However, as exercise went, there was nothing more effective. Jamie knew; she'd tried everything.

The class lined up on the blue mats, Jamie positioning herself behind Stephanie, who was twenty pounds overweight. Working behind Stephanie always made her feel better. On most days she even shouted encouraging, peppy things to Stephanie in her best cheerleader voice, not that Jamie had ever been a cheerleader, but she knew the tone.

Stephanie needed a cheerleader, because she could never execute the ball stretch, a feat which Jamie excelled at. After watching a few of Stephanie's painful not-quite-contortions, Jamie decided to intervene, and spotted her until she got the hang of it.

"You're really good at this torture. Do any S&M in your spare time?" asked Stephanie.

For Jamie, who had no spare time, it was more of a

joke than Stephanie realized. She wiggled her eyebrows. "Just call me Helga."

Stephanie laughed and Jamie warmed inwardly. This was bonding. This was human interaction with absolutely no ulterior motivation.

"How long did it take you to get in shape?" gasped Stephanie, trying to kick her legs over her head.

Jamie kicked her legs over easily. "I've always worked out. Mother started us when we were about six."

"Gymboree?"

"No, Jane Fonda."

Stephanie was suitably impressed, and kicked herself back into a sitting position. Jamie continued to hold the position.

"That's harsh."

"Eh. Mom believed in structure. What was your mother like?"

Stephanie grinned. "She was the best. Cupcakes on Fridays. Huge amounts of icing."

"Chocolate?" asked Jamie, as they rolled onto their backs and began the ab stretching.

"Gobs of it."

"Ladies, ladies, on your breathing. Inhale. Hold, two, three, four."

Jamie counted out an extra four beats before exhaling.

"Don't I see you down here sometimes?" asked Stephanie. "I'm looking for someone who has more motivation than me. Maybe to give me some guidance."

"I don't know," started Jamie and then stopped. Her career might have hit a temporary lull, but she had a date. And with that date would come the compulsive need to analyze, discuss and critique. Discussions were best done with a friend. Ergo, Jamie had to find a friend, preferably before Friday.

"Yeah. I think it'd be good," she said, figuring how she was going to fit Stephanie into her schedule. "Are you up at five?"

Stephanie raised her brows. "A.m.? Are you nuts?"

"Oh. How about six then? I have to be at the office by seven-thirty."

Stephanie didn't look happy, but obviously she sensed she was in the company of a member of the rat race. "I can do six."

Mentally Jamie adjusted her schedule. By kicking in an extra hour at night, she could relax over an elliptical for a while. She gave Stephanie a whack on the back. "It's a plan, my friend. Welcome to hell."

WEDNESDAY DAWNED NORMALLY enough, but soon there was something strange going on in the office. The flock of interns were giggling over a computer screen. Slacker behavior wasn't condoned nor encouraged at Bond-Worthington, and she considered giving them a mentorly heads-up, but then she noticed Helen heading toward the hoi polloi, and Jamie waited for the on-coming collision.

Helen would set them straight.

Or not. Helen's face creaked into a smile, and Jamie's smile faded. While she watched, Helen laughed and pointed and shared in the joke. A joke that excluded Jamie, of course. Because no one thought that she had a sense of humor.

In vain, Jamie waited for Helen—who had been her friend first—to wave her over. The wave never came, and the little lump of envy turned rock-solid.

Not that she cared, of course. Social chitchat and watercooler gossip was for those who escaped the notice of upper management. Such was the blessing of the too young to be laid off, and too under-salaried to be let go.

Jamie kept her nose to the computer screen, googled everything she could about Sandy the Gorgon, and in general, tried to ignore what was going on outside the glass walls of her office.

The laughter carried well through the glass.

As the minutes dragged, she scanned the mechanical green letters on the Bloomberg terminal, searching for trends, conclusions, yet only one kept rearing its ugly head.

Helen was fraternizing with the enemy.

B&W had a stringent caste system in place. Every position had a rank, a behavior, and appropriate office furnishings assigned to it. No one followed the order more closely than Helen, except for maybe Jamie, who had worked her butt off for glass walls and oak trim. Wall Street was a precise, black and white world. Things were neat, orderly, compartmentalized, and measured, and for the life of her, she couldn't figure out what would cause Helen to step out of her box.

The day dragged on and by five o'clock, Jamie was frantic to know the cause. While Helen was closing up shop, Jamie made a casual trip over to Walter's office, pretending she was headed for the break room.

"Going home?" she asked, perching on a desk corner, declaring her intent to practice casual conversation.

Helen looked up and fixed a cheeky hat on her head. "Chicken's on sale at D'Agastinos. Got to hit it right when the night trucks come in."

Jamie nodded like she was an experienced chicken shopper. "Yeah, I saw that. I was going to stop there myself."

Helen, ignoring the workings of a casual non-work-oriented conversation, turned off the desk light and lifted a hand. "See you tomorrow, Jamie. Have a nice evening."

Words sprang to Jamie's tongue, an invitation for a cup of coffee, or maybe a request to hit D'Agastinos, too, but Jamie stopped herself just in time. She had a market wrap-up to create, work to be done, a Gorgon to tame.

No time to finagle secrets.

"You have a nice evening, Helen. Good luck with that chicken," she added, and swung her legs off the desk, heading back in the direction of her office.

Slowly the office emptied out. At exactly seven p.m., the row of VPs filed out, like precision wooden birds on a cuckoo clock. No one dared leave first, and people noticed who left last. Usually Jamie.

Eventually she was all alone on the floor. It wasn't a huge area, B&W marketed themselves as a boutique firm, so they purposefully kept each floor with a minimal number of offices and cubicles. All forty floors worth.

Jamie smiled to herself because she liked the end of the day, liked the hours when the whirr of the computers stopped, and the overhead ticker faded to black. She kicked off her shoes and headed to the vacant corner office, and then looked out over the Hudson. It was a beautiful view, and one she never got tired of. For a luxurious minute she dreamed, thinking that in another three years, this office could be hers. Then the interns could snicker all day, because with one stroke of red ink, she could fix their job prospects permanently. Not that she would—really—unless completely pressed.

So what were they snickering about?

She wandered over to the regulation bunker of intern desks, leaning over Lindsey's computer. There were ways to find out what they had been doing. Technically it would be spying, but in these days of Sarbanes-Oxley, the SEC, and Homeland Security, eyes were watching, recording, logging, and erasing everywhere. She didn't know computers, didn't understand the technology sector, but she knew enough about Internet browsers to be considered dangerous.

She flipped a switch, the machine humming to life.

The firm's logo flashed, and she waited patiently while she logged in with the secret, super-administrator password that everyone knew about. In less than ten clicks of the mouse, she was staring at Lindsey's history file. The usual sites were listed: Women's Wear Daily, E!Online, Reuters and then she found the one that didn't belong.

Just like a treasure hunt.

With a sweeping click, she opened up the Web site.

There were no cartoons, no funny graphics, no, nothing but text. The entries did have one thing in common, though.

Sex.

Scandalous pages of it. Most focused on New York media-types, the poodles and hounds of Manhattan.

Quickly she began to skim, trying to figure out which entry had generated the giggles.

The steamy words slowed her down, a heated flush rising to her face. But there was nothing that might generate giggles—

And then she saw it.

It started at Grand Central, two Wall Street execs, desperate to hop the 9:47 to Connecticut. He was tall, handsome, stuffy in that Mr. Darcy way. She was the investment world's Elizabeth Bennett.

But this wasn't some frigid ballroom in England, this was the overheated New York climate, which had nothing to do with global warming. It didn't take long for two members of the opposite sex to discover a new way to handle the hours-long traffic tie-ups. The Hummer limo had been an impulse, a joke, mostly a mode of transportation. But soon the couple was riding more than I-95. She was buxom and sensual, a Wall Street trader used to dealing in monetary exchanges, not working the carnal side of the market.

She began with a daring disrobing, button by button, her body opening itself to him. His strong hands parted the flimsy silk, palming her breasts, and testing their valuation. His thumbs brushed over her nipples, peaking them instantly. She caught her lip between her teeth at the exquisite torture, swallowing her moan, mindful of the millions of people surrounding them, separated only by the anonymity of privacy glass.

His eyes were so serious, so knowing, as if he could read all her valuations. After all, he was Bull Market Jack, the dark-eyed wizard of Wall Street. "I have to see you," he said, his voice ragged with a passion never seen outside the trading floor. Honey knew she would deny him nothing. She wanted him to see her. For him, for this one moment in time, she was his.

His hands slid up her thigh, under her skirt, pulling the material up over her hips, leaving only a thin, silk barrier that separated her from everything that she knew was wrong. It was so very wrong, so very wicked, but she couldn't resist living in the moment. This moment. His thumbs locked under the thin silk, and slowly, surely he began to slide the single barrier down her thighs. Her heart pounded, the blood flowing from her chest to the secret place between her legs, where the pulse beat thick and heavy. It was desire, pure and simple.

His eyes were black with heat as he waited for

her to stop him, but that moment would never come. Her body was too far gone to stop. Her back arched, melting into him. Then his fingers slipped inside, the moist heat betraying her even further, taking her into paradise…

In the quiet of the office, she could have screamed. But she wouldn't give him the satisfaction. She took a long, shaky breath, letting the red anger seep through her skin. Better anger than desire, right?

Because obviously Bull Market Jack was scum.

Mr. Darcy? *What a crock.*

Still, she knew Andrew hadn't written this. A man who knew P/E ratios, wouldn't know paradise from penny stocks. No, the rat must have talked. Bragging to his buddies about his sexual exploits. Plucked like low-hanging fruit, ripe on the vine.

She sat in Lindsey's chair, still and silent. And used. The interns hadn't known it was her, no one knew it was her, but that was cold comfort. She never trusted men, never believed in anyone but herself, and the one time she stepped off the pier, well, thank heavens that he didn't have a camera. But he'd underestimated who he was tangling with. She was no amateur to be played.

Quietly she packed up her papers to go home— anywhere but here.

All the way to her building in Battery Park, she raged, plotting a public lashing not seen since Elliot Spitzer manhandled the Tyco execs in court. No, the situation called for even more drastic measures. It called for revenge. Tawdry and cheap. Planting underwear on his desk. Or plastic blow-up dolls in his briefcase. Or…

The cab screeched to a stop in front of her building and Jamie slammed a fist on the worn leather seat because after the anger came the pain and *that* was an intervention she dreaded. She didn't do pain well. Had always avoided it as a matter of course. Her father had taught her that pain was for the weak-hearted and Jamie was a McNamara. Stout blood ran in her veins.

Soundlessly she paid off the driver, plodded to her fifth floor apartment, performed a rigorous one-hour workout to her heavy metal playlist, stretching until her tight muscles begged for mercy. Then, without missing a beat, she undressed, jumped into the shower, and for the first time in three years, cried.

"WHAT THE HELL DID YOU DO?" Andrew snarled as soon as the door opened. He threw the print copy in his brother's face.

Jeff opened his apartment door, not looking a bit sorry. "Come on in, now that all my neighbors know you're here."

The righteous attitude was rich, considering that Jeff's parties were notorious—and loud.

Andrew barged in, collapsed on the stuffed leather couch. White, of course.

It wasn't hard to figure out the source. Only a man with a flair for spin, verve and sex could have concocted such an outrageous, partially true and unbearably hot version of the actual events.

Secretly, Andrew knew he had no one to blame but himself. He should have kept his mouth *shut*. Outwardly though, it was his baby brother who was cruising for a fall.

Said baby brother picked up the pages and read them, and then began to laugh. He looked up, the wicked brown eyes dancing. After seeing the white-hot fury in Andrew's face, he collapsed into even further fits of laughter.

"I'm glad you're amused."

"Oh, come on. It's harmless. Hell, you aren't even named, unless you consider the Mr. Darcy bit, and Andrew, that's one clue that *nobody* will ever figure out."

"What if *she* sees it?"

Jeff pulled a shrug. "Maybe she won't know it's her."

"Maybe? Well, hell, maybe the Dow will hit thirty thousand, pigs will fly and the Mets will win the Pennant."

"Might."

"Plug into the real world, Jeff. I could kill you for this one. You've had some huge screw-ups in the past, the Ambassador's daughter, leaving the key to your safety deposit box in the blonde's bra, getting kicked out of Lotus, but this…"

He stopped and leaned his elbows on his knees. Time for the death blow. "You've never cut me like this before."

Jeff sobered up. "I didn't tell anybody."

Andrew pointed to the 8.5 x 11 printout that called him a liar.

"I told Mercedes," Jeff admitted.

Immediately the rat had a face. His sister's face. "Why?"

"She was depressed. Her latest broke up with her on the same day that she got another rejection letter on her novel. I knew it would cheer her up."

Andrew pulled his brother up by the shoulder, and with his free hand, fished out his cell, all the while walking toward the door.

"Where're we going?"

Andrew smiled, cold, calm, back in control. "Can't you guess? I've got a sister to kill."

Mercedes gaped at the Web stats, satisfaction pouring over her, as smooth as good sex. And they said she couldn't write. Her plots were "formulaic." Her characters "unsympathetic." They might be unsympathetic, but they sure knew how to do one thing well. Her own love life might be a solitary, dismal place as of two days ago. But on The Red Choo Diaries? Ha.

The Web site had been a lark. A moment of desperation, and today she earned a mention in the *Wall Street Journal.*

Okay, it wasn't the *New Yorker,* but the road to fiction excellence had to start somewhere.

The buzzer interrupted her moment of glory, and she danced to the wall.

"Who's there?"

"Flowers for Mercedes Brooks."

She recognized her brother's voice and buzzed him up anyway. Jeff was all right for an older brother. Better than—

Andrew.

Her older brother filled her doorway, scowling. It didn't take a mind reader to see he was jacked. It didn't take a genius to figure out why. She huffed. God knows, *his* love life could've used the adrenalin rush. He should be thanking her, down on his knees in gratitude—

"What the hell, Mercedes?"

Not exactly gratitude. She took a defensive step back into the safety of her apartment. "The bears of Broad and Wall got you by the tail, Andrew?"

The bait didn't work. He didn't even blink. Damn, money always worked with Andrew. "What's the problem?" she asked innocently.

Jeff stepped out from behind the hulk. "I told him."

The turncoat. "Bastard," she snapped, because in a perfect world she'd be offered a six-figure deal, roar up the *New York Times* list, and her older brother would have never pulled his head out from the stock boards.

Life really wasn't fair.

She blinked. "I'm sorry," she whispered, and then burst into helpless-little-sister tears.

Her two older brothers, always ready to run to the rescue of every other victim in distress, stood like the uncaring statues they were.

"It won't work," said Andrew, his words clipped and carefully enunciated, which meant he was totally P.O.ed.

She sniffed and peeked up through tear-lined lashes. "It's a piece of fiction," she said in a marvelously weak voice.

"It's my life."

Mercedes finally stopped the act, shock limiting her normally dramatic flair. "You mean it's true?" She pointed to Jeff, who looked guilty as usual. "I thought he made it up. He always makes things up."

Jeff shrugged. "Not this time," he said, before settling himself into her one single metal chair, looking vastly amused. Oh, yeah, for once, he was the innocent party. Not. She turned on him.

"You shouldn't have blabbed."

"You shouldn't have put it on a freaking Web site."

She was too smart to fall for the old shift-the-blame ploy. "Come on. You always make up junk. Remember the one about condom bingo?"

"That happened!" he shot back.

Her lip curdled. "You are such a slut."

Andrew stepped between them. "Excuse me. This is my private life we should be discussing."

Mercedes flipped her long, dark hair back out of her eyes, because it didn't matter what she did, or what she said. Andrew would always be furious at her, and she'd resigned herself to that a long, long, *long* time ago. "I suppose you're not interested in the fact that I got three e-mails from literary agents today."

He didn't even crack a smile. The greatest achievement in her writing career and he didn't even care. "You're shutting it down."

"No," she said, drawing her line in the sand. Normally Andrew's opinion mattered, because well, he was usually financing it. But this time, she'd done it all on her own and Big Bad Bro wasn't going to snatch that away.

"It's my life," he said.

"It's fiction."

He snorted, his cheeks flushed. "You'd exploit me like this? After all I've done for you?"

"Now we get the big 'All I've done' speech. Everybody cue the violins, 'cause I know the words by heart. 'After all I've paid,' isn't that how it goes?"

Some part of her—some deep, secret part of her—felt sorry for Andrew, because when it came to people, family, or feelings, his minimum balance came up to a big fat zero.

She glanced up to see if he was paying attention, but he looked hurt. He actually looked hurt. Andrew never got hurt. He was like some huge, stone colossus with a rock for a heart. But this time…

If only she hadn't seen the numbers on the Web stats, calling to her. Millions of eyes coming to read her writing. If her somewhat trampled ego wasn't flying higher than a kite, she might have felt guilt. Or pity.

"You owe me," he said, just like a heartless stone colossus would. Always reminding her of debts she could never repay. Pity flew out the window.

"Oh, yes, you've paid," she said, getting herself really worked up, because he could rest on *his* laurels, *his* achievements. He'd already made his mark. For the first time, her mark was in sight. She'd made steps. Big steps.

Mercedes lifted an arm, a touch dramatic, but whoop-de-do, she was entitled. "We all know about those golden strings you pull. 'Mercedes, don't do this.' 'Mercedes can't do that.' Well, find another puppet, Andrew. Pinocchio's become a real boy."

"Girl," corrected Jeff.

"Shut up!" she snapped, because Jeff normally didn't have a literary thought in his head.

Andrew stuffed his hands in his pockets, coins and keys clinking ominously. For long seconds he worked his jaw, his eyes fixed stubbornly out the window, a sure sign she'd hit his Achilles heel—mainly because she never missed.

Finally he turned. "You have to delete the entry. Keep the rest of it up, I don't care. It's your reputation. Just keep my name out of it."

And that was the part that infuriated her. "Your name isn't in there."

His jaw worked again. "You know what I mean."

"It's not that easy."

"Of course it's that easy. You select the text and press delete. Here, let me show you."

She stopped him before he got to her computer. "I have fifty e-mails that want to know who Bull Market Jack and the Hummer Honey are. Lehman Brothers is running an office pool and offered me ten percent of the pot if I'd spill. It's gonna be *big*."

"You'd drag me through the gutter for ten percent of an office pool?"

"No one knows it's you," she repeated, because what did it matter?

"She knows."

That stopped her, because her brother never had a weakness for a woman. *Never.* Until now.

Mercedes was touched—marginally. In fact, if Louisa Parker from the Rhinehart Agency hadn't just sent her that e-mail requesting an immediate book proposal, she probably would have conceded.

She did hesitate, though, and Andrew saw the moment of weakness.

"You're not being fair to her, Mercedes. That's her life, too."

"Who is she?" Mercedes asked curiously, realizing this wasn't some bubblegum temp who had seen Andrew's bank account as fair game.

However, Andrew remained stubbornly secret, which meant this wasn't a bubblegum temp. This was something more. Mercedes was intrigued.

"It's like a state secret, highly confidential," answered Jeff.

Immediately, the plot ideas ran like March rain in her mind. She'd thought the woman had worked in Andrew's office, but this was even better. A diplomat, the First Lady, a certain Senator from New York…

Apparently some of the excitement shone in her

eyes, because Andrew stepped in to dam up the flow. "It's not a state secret, she's just an average New York female. Single, and not involved in government service. And that's all I'm going to say."

"She works on Wall Street," added Jeff.

Andrew glared in his direction.

Jeff shrugged. "You're the one who told me."

"I was slightly intoxicated."

Jeff quirked a brow. "As if that's an excuse?"

"You're loving this, aren't you?"

"The ironic justice that for once, the older, more responsible brother really steps in it, big-time? Yeah, yes, I am."

Andrew turned to Mercedes. "Help me."

Helplessly she shook her head. "Bull Market Jack is huge, Andrew. He's a hero to traders everywhere." Then inspiration struck. "Wait. What if I make something up about Honey? Something new, that's obviously a lie, and maybe she'll think it wasn't about her at all? What about that? I can make something up. Jeff can help me."

"Just delete the first entry."

"But then everyone will think it was bogus. I like the adding on a new and improved story. Continuing their sexcapades—"

Andrew winced. Mercedes, having long practiced the art of ignoring him, continued. "—with something new. I have to leave them as financial types, because the *Wall Street Journal* really ate that up. Whole hog. It was great."

"*The Journal?* They wrote about this in the *Journal?*"

Uh oh. "I thought you knew. How did you find out about it?"

Andrew closed his eyes. "They were laughing at the office. Laughing. In the men's room. I was there, tending to my business, and all of a sudden…"

He trailed off, and the sympathy returned like some unkillable pest. It wouldn't be fun for somebody like Andrew to have his love life discussed in the men's room. For Mercedes, it was a goal, a life wish, to be up there, discussed at watercoolers all over America, or at the very least, New York.

Still, this was Andrew, and she needed to remember that. "I can't delete it. It goes to credibility. Unless I get a book deal, and then I'll give you a piece of the action."

"I don't want money," he grated out, a tic in his jaw pulsing. Andrew never had tics before. Her conscience grew two sizes too large, and Mercedes quickly snuffed it out before it could cause permanent damage. "Can I pay you to delete it?"

Mercedes threw her hands up in the air. "No. Can't you understand something besides the almighty dollar? This is about *my career.* People are talking. For the first time, people are reading my stuff. I'll write up a second entry, something outrageous, something so that Mystery Woman will realize that it's not her, or at least it's not her anymore, and you can make it up to her. Has she read it?"

Andrew looked out the window. "I haven't talked to her."

Jeff began to laugh. "Oh, you are in such deep, deep trouble, my friend. You need to call her."

"I didn't want to say anything until I had all the facts."

"She didn't call you?" Mercedes asked. "That means she hasn't read it."

A flash of hope crossed Andrew's face, but quickly it disappeared. "She's not the type to call and chew me out. She's not even the type to call. I had just talked her into a date. One simple date." He looked at Mercedes. "Until all this happened."

Why did he have to look so miserable? "I'm sorry," she said. Mere words, completely useless. "I could talk to her."

"No!"

"It was just an idea."

"A bad idea."

"I'm only trying to help." She went over to Andrew and laid a hand on his arm. As a family they weren't touchy-feely, they squabbled more than average, and they didn't chat at all hours like on the wireless phone commercials, but there was something there. Underneath the bluster, the insults and the arguments, the Brooks family stood together. Because of Andrew, they had survived.

Mercedes blew the stray hair out of her eyes.

"I'll take it out," she said, watching her future on the *New York Times* bestseller list go up in smoke.

"You'd do that?" Andrew asked, almost a smile on his face.

"Yeah. Yes, I would."

He looked in her eyes, dark eyes that looked so much like his, and sighed. "Let me talk to her. If I can fix it, and there's no guarantee I can, I'll see if she'll agree to let you run with the future stuff. Until you create some other Joe Schmo and his—you know—to pick on."

"You'd do that?"

He shrugged. "I know how long you've been chasing this one. I'll try. But no more writing about Jack and Honey until she gives the okay."

She pulled her face into something that looked contrite. "I thought Jeff made the whole thing up. If I'd known it was really true— My God, Andrew? A limo? Come on, you have to tell us who she is. Can we meet her?" She glanced over at Jeff. "Twenty dollars says she's a redhead."

Jeff shook his head. "Nah. Blonde. Only a blonde can make a man go wild."

She glared from underneath night-dark bangs. "Thank you, Jeff."

"Present company excluded, of course."

Andrew cleared his throat. "She's got brown hair."

Mercedes smiled triumphantly. "Works every time."

Her older brother, near, possibly dear, and most of the time a real stick in the mud, pulled up Jeff and pushed him out the door. "I'm getting out of here before it gets worse."

Jeff grinned. "You really have to learn to keep your mouth shut, Drew."

Andrew socked him in the back. "You are such a putz."

6

THE FIRST LILY ARRIVED at 8:00 a.m. the next morning. It was white, long-stemmed, and accompanied by a card, signed only "A." At 8:30, another one arrived, same setup, same card. Eventually Jamie was surrounded with twenty-four lilies, twelve cards (they started coming in boxes of two's at 10:00) and one funeral wreath shaped like a horseshoe, with the letters "A-N-D-R-E-W" spelled out in red chrysanthemums.

He made it very difficult to plot out revenge that involved bodily harm. He really did. She hadn't settled on a final plan, mainly because the next morning, when the interns gathered around the monitors, Jamie knew it was her they were envying, her love life they were tossing around so casually. Heck, even the *New York Times* had mentioned that the Hummer limo had became the number one requested car in New York. They didn't know why.

Jamie did.

All the anonymous attention was starting to go to her head. The white lilies drew her eyes like a magnet,

and she traced the soft, blood-red petals of the chrysanthemums. The soft flowery scent tickled her nose
and she wheeled her chair back to the safety of her
desk. Why couldn't he have been a jerk? A typical
male who never called, never apologized, and never
occupied another second of her thoughts.

What had been a heart-breaking betrayal was now
a mystery. Yeah, so her sex life had been plastered all
over the Internet. It wasn't that awful when nobody
knew it was you.

Jamie stretched against the chair back, and stared
mindlessly at her computer screen. Okay, she wasn't
going to completely forgive him, but she did rule out
sending over the transvestite stripper. No, she was
going to listen to him, assuming their date was still on,
and considering the flora in her office, she suspected
that it was.

Walter walked by, noticed the flowers, and did a
double take. Jamie tried not to preen, but it was hard.

"You're a popular lady today."

A blush tiptoed up her cheeks, but she maintained a
professional calm. "Just a good friend, playing a joke."

Walter's brows lifted above the rims. "I see."

Jamie took the hint: personal business was not
allowed. All Bond-Worthington, all the time. "The
Russians are tanking the oil market. We should study
the Venezuelan market, they'll be the ones most likely
to benefit."

He nodded once, briskly. High praise indeed. "I'll
get Floyd on it. Any word from Newhouse?"

Jamie's smile was forced. "Not yet. I've got to handle him very carefully. Don't want to look too eager," she answered, as if two calls a week for the last three months was dragging her feet.

"Don't wait too long. The second quarter will be up soon. And then where will we be? Stuck in the final game of the series, do or die, two outs, three on base." He wagged his finger at her. "I'm counting on you, McNamara."

"I won't let you down," she said, putting her hand on the phone, ready to battle the Gorgon again.

"I know," he said, and then went on his way, chuckling at some unknown joke.

Her phone rang, and she picked it up. If there was a career goddess, it would be the Gorgon, returning her call.

"I'm sorry," he said.

Andrew.

The scourge of her existence (and fantasies), the man who had sullied her reputation (anonymously), the ogre who had sent her flowers (ahhhh).

What was it about his voice that made her smile? She really didn't know, but the recording industry should really figure out how to capture it and use it, possibly in cars, elevators, or answering machines. America would be a happier place. "I figured it was you," she answered, twirling the cord around her finger, before she realized what she was doing. She slapped her hand on the desk.

"You're still talking to me?"

She straightened up in her chair, ramrod posture, thighs locked together. Distance. Discipline. Determination. "What happened?" she asked curtly, not going to be swayed by a mere bunch of flowers, cute as they were.

"No one knows that it's you. No one," he stressed.

"I was shocked when I read it," she said. "Shocked," she repeated for good measure.

"So you've seen it, then?"

"Yes, just like the rest of Wall Street. Tomorrow they'll want the Hummer Honey to ring the opening bell."

She studied her nails, cool as a cucumber, proud of the spotless manicure. Rigorous attention to detail kept everything as it should be, including men.

Muffled laughter rumbled on the other end. "Sorry," he muttered.

"You owe me an explanation," she said, getting back to the script she'd prepared in her head.

He sighed into the phone. "I went out drinking with my brother. He was giving me a hard time. I don't get out much," he said, by way of explanation.

"And?" she prodded.

"I said a couple of things. But I didn't tell him who you are. Normally, I swear I never say anything, and I give you my word, it won't happen ever again."

"I should hope not," she said primly, back to twirling her finger in the cord. "Your brother writes The Red Choo Diaries?"

"Not exactly," he answered.

"So he told someone else?" she asked, not liking where this was leading.

"My sister."

"Oh, God," Jamie muttered. "You must have a very creative family."

"Not really. But I talked to her. She sends her apologies by the way."

"And she'll remove the text?"

"I wanted to talk to you about that," he started.

"Why?" asked Jamie tightly.

"She's gotten a lot of press from the story, and people want to read more."

"Well, too bad," answered Jamie.

"And that's the last of you and me, of course, but the fictional characters…"

"What fictional characters?"

"Jack and Honey."

"What about Jack and Honey?"

"She'd like to continue using them. Just, you know, making things up, of course. No one would ever know."

"Except your family," she said, horrified at the thought.

"Well, yes, but just my brother and sister."

"Not your mother and father?"

"My father left when I was a kid."

"I'm sorry," she said automatically, and then quashed the short spurt of sympathy. She needed to stay tough, on message. "Surely you didn't tell your mother?"

"Oh, God, no."

"Thanks for small miracles."

"You're mad?"

"Yes," she said, looking at the red polish and thinking that maybe she should change her signature color to something softer. Like pink, for instance.

He laughed awkwardly. "Let's talk about something nice, pleasant, non-stress inducing. Are we still on for tomorrow?"

Oh, he knew how to make it difficult for her. She wanted to say no and teach him a lesson. Show him that Jamie McNamara couldn't be pushed around, but he was appealing, in a mouthwatering manner.

He wasn't arrogant like the peculiar male species that roamed Wall Street. Most of them were full of overblown egos, and market insight they believed was direct from the Fed. Mistakes were not admitted, fingers were pointed across the table, and apologies were seen as a sign of weakness.

Andrew was oddly humble. If she had to guess, he was probably just starting out at some Betty Sue Brokerage house. A date wouldn't be bad; in fact, she might be able to give him some advice. Her rationale sounded reasonable, well-intentioned.

Yeah, if you bought that…

"This won't be fodder for your sister's scintillating sex stories, will it?" she asked, because weak as she may be, she wasn't stupid.

"Of course not," he replied immediately. "Jack and Honey are completely fictional from now on."

"Good. You aren't planning on going out drinking with your brother anytime soon?"

"Never again. Swear."

"Well, maybe that's a little extreme. So, yes, I'll agree to go out with you tomorrow. See you at eight?"

"I'm looking forward to it."

Jamie cleared her throat efficiently. "See you then," she said and then hung up.

Shortly thereafter she did a Snoopy dance in her office, taking care to make sure that no one was watching.

THE NEW WOMAN IN 43C loved rhinestones. The first time Andrew saw the new tenant, he had to blink from the rays of light that shined from her. It was like looking into the setting sun with mirrors on two sides, all without sunglasses. She had emerged from her apartment, and once his sight had been restored, he'd found himself face to face with what Old Lady Feldman had now termed The Tramp. Andrew wasn't that judgmental, although she definitely was wearing some miles. Her face had the tanned, weathered skin of a Florida smoker, although her eyes were nice. The skintight blue jeans encased skinny legs and an absence of butt. He nodded courteously, and she shot him a completely un-harloty look. "Good evening," she said in a husky voice. Andrew didn't think she was coming on to him, but Old Lady Feldman's stories weighed heavy on his brain, so in record time he unlocked his apartment and escaped inside.

It was some time later when his doorbell rang.

"Mr. Brooks?"

Old Lady Feldman.

After he invited her in, she settled on his couch, adjusting her skirt and feet just so. He smiled, trying to make her feel comfortable. Not his forte, but he tried. She was nice, in a gossipy, Puritan sort of way.

"What can I do for you?"

"43C," she started, then narrowing her eyes like he was supposed to deduce everything from an apartment number.

"Is there a problem?" he asked, because although 43C seemed to like her clothes with bling, she didn't play loud music, had no barking dogs, and never flooded her place. In Andrew's book, that made her a winner.

"Of course there's a problem," the older woman snapped, and Andrew realized that he and Estelle Feldman valued different qualities in floor mates.

"It's the men. Coming and going. All hours of the night. I can't sleep, what with all the door openings and closings, and you know what goes on behind closed doors."

"Perhaps she's just sociable," answered Andrew, who knew exactly what went on behind closed doors and highly encouraged it. He wasn't dead yet. Besides, the last tenant in 43C had been a lady drummer with a taste for Jimi Hendrix. Loud Jimi Hendrix.

Old Lady Feldman started knotting her hands together, lips quivering, and in general making him feel like a snot. All because he didn't care about what someone did privately, as long as he couldn't hear it.

"Do you expect me to do something?" he asked, a stupid question because he knew the answer. Andrew went to school with the head of the building's board, and everyone in the building knew that Boone Slager sat in Andrew's pocket. Mainly because when the building's AC had needed revamping, Andrew had provided the cash.

The old lady looked up at him with those trusting, cocker spaniel eyes. "I don't think there's anything anyone can do. I just worry. With those muggings in Sutton Place now, if Sutton Place isn't safe anymore, who knows what sort of fiddle-faddle can trouble an old woman like me."

Somewhere in the darkness of his heart, violins began to play. Andrew was, by nature, cynical. It happened about the time his bank account hit ten zeros. But the trusting look in the old woman's eyes, well, he might be cynical, but he wasn't a schlep.

"I'm sure there are things we can do. I'll check into it." Then he reached over and patted her hand. "Don't worry, Mrs. Feldman."

"It's Miss," she said with a sniff. "I was going to get married once, but my Henry died in Korea before he made it back home."

Andrew suspected that Henry had saved himself about forty years of misery, but he bit his tongue. "Look, I hate to run out on you, but I have to be across town in less than half an hour."

Old Lady Feldman creaked up from the couch and then toddled to the door. "Thank you, Mr. Brooks."

"I'll take care of everything," he promised, because nobody handled problems better than Andrew. Nobody.

ON FRIDAY, ANDREW MADE it to Jamie's building ten minutes early. CPI reports or not, there was no way he was going to be late tonight. At one minute to eight, he saw her come off the elevator into the lobby.

He didn't want to grin or look too eager, so he stuffed his hands in his pockets and pretended to study the marble squares.

Her high heels clicked efficiently on the marble, and just that noise, the brisk tick-tick of her approach, made him hard. God, he was a dweeb, or else just now discovering some seriously perverted sexual fantasies. He wasn't sure which was worse.

Quickly he found his composure, until her high heels came into view. They were red. Scarlet. The color of lipstick, nail polish, and engorged female parts—

Andrew mentally slapped himself, and lifted his gaze from her heels—slowly, though. He wasn't missing a moment of this. She had a glorious form. Long, muscled legs covered in shadowy stockings. Lush hips poured into a black skirt. And the breasts— it didn't matter that she was wearing a suit jacket and a white linen blouse. Nothing could hide those large cap curves.

He forced himself to smile.

She wasn't smiling back. Her briefcase was clutch- ed to her stomach, and basically, Jamie McNamara looked furious.

His smile fell two points. "Thank you."

That seemed to take her off guard. "For what?"

"For allowing me to live."

She laughed, and he relaxed. "I did bring you something."

It was his turn to be confused. "What?"

She pulled a lily out of her briefcase and brushed it across his chest. It wasn't supposed to be a sexy gesture, but like a Rorschach inkblot test, he kept seeing flashes of her—bare and breathless—in the most inopportune places. He caught the flower before it did further damage.

"I'm sorry," he repeated.

"You've already apologized once."

"I'm sure I'll apologize again before the night is over."

"Where're we going?"

He took her briefcase, wanted to take her arm, but decided that the ever-prickly Jamie wasn't ready for such a forward move, and motioned for the door.

"The restaurant's down on the water. We can walk," he glanced at the heels, winced, "or take a cab."

"I'd like to walk, please," she answered, probably not willing to trust him in the confines of a moving vehicle ever again.

They walked alongside the West Side Highway, a night breeze from the river kicking up the dust in the air. Andrew wasn't ready for casual conversation, most of his conversations were pertaining to all things financial, yet he didn't want to talk finance with Jamie tonight. The breeze had cooled him down, both literally and metaphorically, and he realized how long it'd been since he'd simply gone for a walk in the city. It was nice, comfortable.

Her long legs ate up the distance quickly, matching

him stride for stride. Once she stumbled, her heel catching in a grate, and he caught her arm, the fleeting touch a hot, hard burn. He heard her indrawn breath, and quickly let her go.

The nice, comfortable silence was gone.

A few minutes later they arrived at Cappy's, an old-style seafood place with lots of wood planking and portholes for windows. The atmosphere wasn't four stars, but the food was, and Andrew spent some time researching a place that was innocent, non-confrontational, and would inspire an intimate evening of quiet conversation. Cappy's seemed about right.

The waitress seated them at a booth in the back, and Andrew was grateful for the shadows that could mask so many things.

Jamie held up the menu like a shield, and he knew then they had a lot of ground to make up. Somewhere along their walk, the rapport had solidified into a full-blown recession, and side-stepping recessions was a job for the Fed, not a mere mortal of a fund manager.

"Are you still mad about the story?" he blurted out.

Her menu lowered. "Yes," she said, and then promptly raised it again.

"I thought we'd gotten past that."

Her menu lowered. "I've changed my mind. I shouldn't have caved in to your charming gestures so easily," she said, promptly raising it yet again.

His heart warmed at the idea that this particular female considered any of his gestures charming. It was an adjective rarely used to describe him, and he didn't understand why one word would mean so much. She had intruded in his carefully ordered life without realizing it. How could she be expected to know that he spent two hours finding a restaurant, bribing the manager for the exact perfect table rather than meeting with Bob from United Banks, who was a huge investor, but a complete blowhard?

And how would she know about the sleepless nights when he dreamed she was beside him, underneath him, her bare skin bathed in Manhattan moonlight? Seven days he had known her, and seven nights he had dreamed of her. Slowly his brain was turning to mush. He needed her in his bed to exorcise some of the lust, before his work started to suffer.

The waitress brought over a bottle of Pellagrino and poured two glasses. He took a long sip, easing the panic inside him. Lust was an emotion for Jeff, Mercedes, and other less responsible human beings. Andrew didn't normally lust; there wasn't one hot-blooded cell in his body.

Until now. Now he was succumbing to some disease, the poetic, heart-pounding, cock-stirring, blood-pumping emotion that the romantics described. And Andrew didn't feel comfortable with emotion, he didn't feel comfortable with lust. Hell, he couldn't get comfortable with casual conversation.

It must mean that he was having a midlife crisis, early. It made perfect sense. He had achieved his life goals at age thirty-one, and now he must be experiencing some deep-seated desire for purpose and meaning, which was manifesting itself through a need to touch Jamie McNamara, strip off her clothes, and thrust himself inside her until his vision blurred.

Okay, it didn't make sense, but the other alternative was too frightening, so Andrew stuck on point. This was a temporary aberration, one he needed to work through, like a stomach virus, and then after that, his life would return to normal.

Because if this mind-numbing emotional roller coaster didn't go away, God help them all.

JAMIE PRETENDED TO STUDY the words in front of her, but she couldn't prevent the small smile on her lips. Part of her wanted to just lay down and forgive him, let him have his evil way with her (or at least she hoped that was the plan), and forget that she was Jamie McNamara, last of the line, strongest of the strong. However, try as she might, she couldn't forget her own name, couldn't forget the lectures and anecdotes and motivational techniques she'd been subjected to in her formative years.

When she had been ten, she'd committed her first serious offense. Her mother had stared at a cavity showing on the dental X-rays and gasped. Her blue eyes turned to Jamie, welling with disappointment. "How could you?" she'd asked.

And Jamie knew it was because she'd been sneaking three chocolate bars at lunch every week for the entire spring semester, ever since Angelina Sherwood had thought she was allergic to chocolate, and would die if she ate another one. It was a dire prediction that perhaps *Jamie* had encouraged.

However, after the dental exam in her mother's office, seeing the disappointment in her mother's face, the black spot on the X-ray like the black spot on her own heart, Jamie had sworn off chocolate bars.

And in the end, she'd lost an extra seven-point-five pounds as bonus. It was a lesson that had lasted a lifetime. Temptation had consequences.

Andrew was a walking, talking six foot tall chocolate bar. He tasted mighty good, but she'd already been burned once. And what self-respecting woman would actually consider making love to a man who had broadcast their exploits over the Internet?

Well, accidentally broadcast their exploits over the Internet. And to be fair, he had been drinking at the time, and he hadn't expected his brother to—

There she went. Already drifting into dangerous water. Quickly Jamie transitioned her thoughts to something that would keep her focus, namely his humble brokerage environs. "Where do you work?"

"I'm at Shearson, Brooks, Panhower and Bloom."

Okay, not Betty Sue's We Buy Stocks, not even close. Jamie tried not to look impressed, but failed. SBPB was the Big Dog. Their exploits, their returns, their cunning contrarian strategies had placed them ahead of even the legendary Berkshire Hathaway in the past down-market years.

Shearson, Brooks, Panhower and Bloom?

Oh, man, she began to develop the vapors just

thinking about it. The firm had been founded by two Yale grads, aka spoiled frat boys, who hired two Harvard MBAs, and the legend grew from there. She studied Andrew carefully, trying to ignore the sexy as all get-out mouth, the intriguing dimple. Instead, she tried to imagine him striding down the marble hallway, talking interest rates, P/E ratios, and futures with the stuffed-shirt titans of SBPB.

Oddly enough, the picture didn't compute. Maybe he was a research analyst? That she could imagine. With that laser-guided attention to detail, he'd found the sensitive skin on the back of her thigh, an erogenous zone she didn't even know she had.

Getting overheated again, Jamie. Shake it off.

"It must be exciting to be in a place with all that positive energy. They're about the only firm that's done respectable in the post-9/11 marketplace," she said, which sounded crisp and businessy, as if she didn't want to jump his bones.

He shrugged and looked away. "They've done okay," he said, and the waitress came and interrupted, taking their order and completely shutting down the conversation.

However, Jamie wouldn't let him off that easy.

"What are the partners like?" she asked, mentally comparing them to stuffy old VP's at Bond-Worthington. Men who thought that a risk was a four-letter word. Two years ago, she'd read a profile on SBPB in *Forbes,* and she still remembered the picture of Andrew—

Brooks—

Oh. My. God.

She bit her tongue, tasted blood in her mouth.

Guilt flared in his face. Instantly she knew that he knew that she knew.

"You're him!" she said accusingly. It was worse than she imagined. He was the hottest manager in Manhattan right now, and hadn't even bothered to tell her. Hell, they'd—and—and for God's sake, she'd seen his—!

"Who is 'him' and I'll tell you if you're right or not," he said coyly.

"You're Andrew Brooks," she said tightly, the full ramifications of her actions finally sinking in.

Oh, my God, she'd slept with Andrew Brooks.

In a Hummer.

For the first time in her life, Jamie felt faint. This *so* wasn't fair. Her first instinct was flight. She got up, ready to bolt out the door, until he put his hand on her arm.

"Don't go," he said, dark eyes pleading with her.

And oh, she didn't want to go. Why wasn't he fat, or ugly, or have big, acne scars on his cheeks? Then at least their positions would have been equal. Instead, he was—The Man.

"I need to go," she said, shaking her head sadly. She might be disciplined, but even a McNamara couldn't resist—him. She wasn't that strong, or that naive.

"Why?"

"That's not fair," she muttered.

"I asked you out on a date. I think I'm entitled to know why who I am should make a difference."

She moved her arm until they weren't touching anymore. She couldn't think when he touched her. "I remembered an earlier scheduled appointment," she lied.

"You're lying."

"Yes."

"What if I was just some mail room flunky, would you still go out with me?"

"No," she answered honestly.

That made him laugh. "You're a snob."

"Yes, yes, I am."

"So I'm not good enough?"

"That's not the problem and you know it."

"What is the problem?"

She sat down in her seat, realizing that she wasn't going to cut and run, but she had to make him understand. "I'm a very ambitious person."

"Yes, it's one of the reasons I like you."

She wanted to ignore the warm fuzzy that gave her, but a small smile played on her lips. "Each of us have a position in our place of employ. I'm not at your level—yet, and I'm not sure I could talk to you, interact with you, and—other things, and forget who you are."

"I don't want you to forget who I am," he said easily.

"Oh, yeah, so you can use your position to keep me in my place?"

"No," he said, his voice laced with irritation. "Because I want you to know me, to like me, to respect me, and my career is everything that I am. You of all people should understand that."

She sighed, because she did understand. *"Why couldn't you be middle management?"*

He took the salt shaker in his hands, twirling it back and forth. "We're both who we are. It doesn't have to be a problem, unless you make it one."

He was so clueless about the ways of the world. Men always had it easy, gliding through life, not fighting against stereotyped expectations, instead zipping along on the Autobahn of business, whereas women were shown the exit ramp at every opportunity.

"You're a man," she whispered quietly, finally. She needed them to be equals and they weren't.

"I didn't realize that would be a problem, unless you're a lesbian and forgot to tell me."

"We're supposed to be equals."

The salt shaker came down with a thump. "No, we're not. That whole 'all men are created equal' is a load of crap. Everyone has different talents, looks, achievements, personalities, and some of those things will get your foot in the door, and some of those things will get the door slammed in your face."

The waitress appeared with a tray full of food, and Jamie used the time to collect her thoughts. Secretly she watched him, watched the legendary Andrew Brooks, and knew she would never trade in the accounts he did.

Eventually the waitress left, and Andrew looked at her expectantly.

Damn.

"If all that you're saying is true, why should I even try?" she asked.

"Because you're you. Because you're Jamie McNamara, client services manager extraordinaire, the talented woman who snagged Adam Maynard, who got Liam Peters to back down from a frivolous lawsuit, and who graduated first in her class at Wellesley."

"You know all that?"

"A fund manager lives and dies by his research."

She gulped down her wine and drank Andrew's as well. "Why didn't you tell me?"

"You didn't tell me your last name at first, either. You were all about the privacy thing. I respect that, and I thought I should do the same."

"You didn't want me to know your last name?"

He frowned. "No. I just didn't want you to feel uncomfortable that you didn't want me to know your last name."

"Very clever," she muttered.

"Not really. I was trying to be," he searched for words, "charming."

Finally she dared to look into the eyes of the man who had been profiled in *Forbes,* had his name on the door of one of Wall Street's most prestigious firms, whose year-end bonus was more than her annual salary. The dark eyes were anxious, unamused, and sincere. Her heart rate slowed to its normal one-twenty beats per minute.

"I know I've screwed up—at least once, possibly twice," he told her. "If it'll help you even things out, take my plate of scampi and dump it all over me."

As if it were that easy. He seemed sincere. He actually seemed sincere. "I can't do that."

"You want everything to be even and fair. I'm just giving you a chance."

He didn't know how tempting it was. A moment to rail against the glass ceiling that could only be broken with a penis. Her fingers even clasped the edges of her own plate. But then she let go. "I can't."

He took a bite of shrimp, happy, well-adjusted, content in his own testosterone-ness. "I think it'll make you feel better."

Then he smiled.

Easily, in a condescending way, as if her anger was a momentary bout of PMS. Little did he know that her anger had been festering for ten years, since her first boss had passed her over for a promotion in favor of one Sam Brody who had slid by with a 2.13 from Yale. She knew his GPA for a fact because she had bribed an intern in HR to look at his transcripts. Numbers didn't lie. The numbers never lied.

In honor of Sam Brody, and all the other women who had submitted wordlessly to second place, Jamie rose, took Andrew's plate, and pressed the contents of his dinner against the perfectly starched white shirt.

He didn't miss a beat. "I thought you'd feel better."

She couldn't help it. She laughed.

AFTER THAT, THE REST OF THE dinner passed quietly. The manager had apologized profusely, as if his staff had been responsible for some culinary faux pas. He rounded up a Cappy's T-shirt from the counter. It was a little small on Andrew, but Jamie didn't mind a bit. The man was ripped.

All she needed to do was forget his last name, his firm, his reputation, and his years of experience. No, she just needed to concentrate on the fact that she was sitting across the table from a gorgeous man who seemed to enjoy her conversation (when they were actually conversing), and best of all, who had the most magnificent mouth that she'd ever had a chance to kiss.

"We've had a rough go of it, haven't we?" he said in a husky voice, and inched his hand across the table. He didn't touch her; he wasn't going to, waiting for her to move first. Her finger inched closer, still not touching his hand, but signifying intent.

This time his hand moved, covering hers completely. "I'm very sorry, Jamie. I wish I could turn everything back, and do this normally."

"It would've been nice," she said, which was somewhat of a lie. She'd been down the normal route before. Forty-five minute lunches, phone calls to say she'd be late, coming home to seven messages on her answering machine telling her she'd missed their date—AGAIN.

The quintessential dating experience was overrated in Jamie's book. She liked the mystery and spontaneity of the situation between Andrew and herself. If you didn't plan a sensual rendezvous, you couldn't be late for it, and she suspected that Andrew wouldn't stand for her being late. Then she remembered the way he had lingered around her thigh and knew in her heart of hearts that she'd be dead before she would ever be late for a sensual rendezvous.

A hot flash bloomed in her privates, as she remembered the feel of him inside her. She wanted to feel that thrill again.

So once more—only the second time in roughly twenty-five years, to be fair—Jamie found herself falling into the trap of temptation.

She shot him an easy smile. "You shouldn't have told me to do that. You were just inviting trouble."

"You don't like being told what to do, but you always follow instructions, don't you?"

"When I want to," she answered primly, but he was right, even if she'd never admit it in a million years. "You thought I'd do it?"

"I'd hoped you would."

"You're a big man, Andrew Brooks."

He shot her a smile over scampi. "I hate what my siblings—what I—did to you. Honestly I've been more of a schmo than usual."

"Why?"

"I don't know," he answered, but his glance dropped to her mouth.

"I got a kick out of reading the story," she whispered, not exactly a come-on, and certainly not something you'd hear in a porn flick, but as talking dirty went, this was her limit.

He looked startled. "You did?"

She nodded. Once.

Then he smiled. A real smile. The honest and warm

smile of a man who could send funeral lilies before a date. Maybe he was Andrew Brooks, but for tonight he was *her* Andrew Brooks.

Then he started to talk. Slowly, like he was searching for words. "I would have killed her if she had named names, I just want you to know that. Even if she is my sister. But she's a good writer."

"It was very spicy," contributed Jamie.

"Yes, yes, it was," he said, and cleared his throat.

They ordered coffee and dessert and that was the end of the discussion, but the thought was there, she knew it. Andrew knew it, too, she could read it in his look. Oh, he was a complete gentleman, courteous, attentive, polite. A great listener. But his eyes would linger more on her than on his plate, flickering to her mouth, her breasts, and she could feel the tingling in her thighs.

They ate and talked and lingered over coffee and chocolate molten lava cake. When Jamie caved, she did it in style. As the minutes ticked past, and the rest of the restaurant grew quiet and still, the tension in her only increased.

She had always thought herself rather mature in dealings of a sexual matter. She wasn't a virgin, hadn't been since the night of her senior prom, along with 83.6 percent of the girls in her senior class. But sex had always been matter-of-fact, a mutually advantageous merger of two bodies, combining for a momentary release of pleasure. There wasn't a buildup, although foreplay was nice, but it usually put her behind schedule.

Andrew muddled it all. She wished she could just

take the bull by the horns, so to speak, and come right out and ask about his intentions for the night. But no matter how she practiced them in her head, the words remained unspoken.

"Can I ask you something?" he asked, his spoon stirring slowly in his coffee.

"Yes," she answered.

He blew out a breath, and rose. "Thank God."

She blinked in surprise, and then realized *the question* had been asked and answered. She smiled, nay, grinned, realizing that great minds did think alike.

Andrew held out a hand, and she hesitated, but not for long. Her pink-hued fingers slipped into his while she struggled to maintain a mature, sophisticated demeanor. Her toes curled up uncomfortably inside her Jimmy Choo's (shoes not meant for toe-curling, by the way).

He rushed her outside, toward the first open cab. When they were safely inside the vehicle, she was intensely conscious of his hand gripping hers, cutting off most of the blood flow, but she didn't mind.

The pain distracted her from the most blood-thumping thought of all. Jamie McNamara was going to make mad, passionate love with Andrew Brooks. And this time, they were going to make it to a bed.

7

THERE HAD BEEN SIX GREAT achievements in Andrew's life. His acceptance to Yale, his graduation, the first day he walked through the Pit, the Dow 10,000, his first million and his first billion. He could remember the smells, the faces of the people around him, the rush in his blood, as if someone had broadcast those days in high definition.

And now there was another to add to the list. He was going to bed Jamie McNamara—again. As the cab zoomed up the FDR, he sat silent, his cock prodding impatiently against his thigh. He could smell her in the cab, the odd essence of things that made up Jamie. She didn't smell flowery, soapy or fruity. She smelled of woman, a rich, musky ambrosia that he would remember for the rest of his life.

The sound of her breathing, low and even, filled the small space, and he remembered the morning on the Connecticut turnpike, the sound of her breathing in his ear, low and even. Until the moment when she came.

His cock stirred again, and this time he let go of her hand. Touching her, *without* really touching her, was a first-rate tease, and Andrew didn't handle teasing well.

When they came upon a lane closure and traffic stalled, Andrew nearly beat the driver. Jamie swallowed a giggle, obviously not enduring the same painful, ball-busting erection he was going through.

Sometimes women really had it easy.

His hand moved, creeping towards the secret heat between her thighs, mainly to torment her, but at the last moment, he stopped, horrified at the idea of pawing her in the back seat of the cab. It was disrespectful, it was crass, and mostly, the last time he'd had Jamie in the back seat of a vehicle, it'd been broadcast to the entire Net universe, courtesy of the *Wall Street Journal*.

The cabbie blew the horn when the car in front of them didn't budge.

"Move your freakin' car," the driver yelled out the window.

A bead of sweat formed on the back of Andrew's neck.

Jamie turned toward him, her smile tight with frustration.

"Sometimes I hate New York," he muttered, wishing he could find something to take his mind off sex. *Work.* Work always took his mind off sex. "You're trying to get the Newhouse account away from Goldman?"

Jamie looked surprised at the new topic, and she hesitated answering. "You know a lot."

"Personality disorder. It's very useful in the trade."

"Yeah, Bond-Worthington wants Newhouse. With

the cash he's sitting on, he should be earning serious returns, not the pennies that he's getting. If I can just get on his calendar, I think I can get it. Goldman-Sachs isn't worthy to lick Bond-Worthington's heels."

"I could call in a marker if you'd like."

He might as well have doused her in cold water, the chill abundantly clear. "I don't think I need your help."

He held up his hands, innocent bystander style. It was a look he'd learned from Mercedes. "No offense intended," he told her. "But it's hard if you're going to go it alone. I've collected my share of people doing favors for me."

"I'm sure."

"It's part of the biz, nothing more. The whole world runs on the 'scratch my back, I won't stab yours' system. You should learn to play."

"I don't need anyone's help," she answered stiffly.

Oh, he remembered those naive days when he thought he could do it all, but it was obvious now wasn't the time to try and educate her on the basic rules of a market-based economy. "If you change your mind, the offer still stands."

She gave him a nod. Once. Message delivered. Hell will freeze first. Okay, good one, Andrew. Wonderful way to end a date.

Soon enough the cabbie delivered them to his Upper East Side condo. He looked at her, a question in his eyes, not sure if she'd still be amendable to easing his misery.

"I can drop you off at your place, if you'd like." He didn't want her to think he wanted her to go home, but he didn't want her to think he was an obnoxious prick, either.

"With my luck, they'll have closed down the FDR entirely. I'll stay here, thanks."

Polite. Succinct. Stubborn. Just like him.

God he loved that.

When they got to his building, the doorman greeted them. Andrew whisked Jamie into the elevator before she could change her mind.

"Nice elevator," she said, her eyes taking in the four steel walls.

"It's home," he answered.

There was a quiet, awkward silence between them, the liquid tension making thirty-six floors seem more like thirty-six thousand. But eventually they were there. At his place.

He wasn't a hermit, had had females at his condo before, but he had never experienced this huge over-whelming feeling of fear. He was terrified she would run, terrified that he would say the wrong thing, and mostly terrified that she wouldn't let him taste her again.

Andrew hated needing people because the only person you could completely depend on was yourself. *He* was the person that people needed, not the other way around. Yet his attitude toward Jamie was fast morphing into need, and he suspected that tonight, making love with her would send him past the point of no return.

But tonight his body and his heart were in charge. Tomorrow he could worry about the doubts.

When he opened the door, she walked inside, her heels clicking on the tile at the entryway. It was like a shot to his brain, the small sound, driving him right out of his mind. He took her in his arms and began to kiss her, just like he'd waited to do all night.

And good things came to those who wait. Her arms curled around his neck, exactly where they belonged. Her lips fell into the kiss as if they'd been together for a thousand years.

Quietly they stood alone in the darkness, tasting, exploring, doing all the things that normal lovers were supposed to do. Andrew pulled her closer, fitting her body to his. Jamie McNamara, normally hell on heels, was purring like a kitten. He'd done that to her.

Determined to be slow, Andrew nibbled on her throat, finding the pulse, feeling the slow beat of her blood.

His hand slid down to cup her rear and that was when, from the living room, he heard discreet coughing.

Not his.

Not hers.

"Andrew?"

It was the most difficult thing he'd ever done, to push Jamie out of his arms, but he managed. He flicked on the lights and they all jumped from the brightness.

He, Jamie—

And his mother.

"Mom?"

Jamie gasped. "This is your mother?"

Now, normally Andrew didn't believe in fate, didn't believe in luck. In his line of work, that only brought sleepless nights. Hell, he didn't even worry on the anniversary of Black Tuesday. But *this?* After all the work he'd done to get Jamie into his life? *For one simple date?*

"Why are you here? And who let you up?" he said, more of a groan than actual words.

Althea Brooks was not a tall woman. In fact, she looked just like a mother. Which at the moment, wasn't exactly what Andrew wanted in his visual range.

"I brought you a present," she answered and gave him a box, gift wrapped in pink paper. "And who is this young lady?" she said to Jamie.

"None of your business, Ma. And if you'll excuse us," he said, marching her towards the door.

"Andrew," said Jamie and his mother in unison.

"What?" he asked, then sighed, seeing that neither woman was going to make this easy. "Mother, can I talk to you in private?"

His mother, immune to the idea of privacy, maturity, and the whole "leaving the nest" concept, looked near to tears. Since his mother was an aspiring actress, this wasn't the five-hanky emotion-fest it should have been.

He pulled her into his study where she could emote as much as she wanted.

"You're always pushing me away."

"What's the audition for now, Ma?" he asked, giving up the idea of a sensual feast on Jamie McNamara's ripe flesh. He cursed his entire family and fell back into a leather armchair.

His mother ignored his pain. "They're casting a movie. De Niro. There's a part for the neighbor, an older woman, well-preserved, but nothing splashy." She patted her hair, still pouffed out in the same style she'd worn as long as Andrew could remember. "I'd be perfect." Then she leaned in close and whispered, "My agent told me I need new head shots. Something more up-to-date." She began to wring her hands. "I tried to talk him out of it, but, he's so much like you, levelheaded, sensible."

It was an argument they'd had over and over, and no matter how hard he'd tried, his mother had refused to believe that her "agent" was actually running a con. His mother, an actress? Yeah, right.

If the world had been a fair and just place that Andrew wanted to believe in, the Brooks family would have been graced with a strong matriarch after their father ran off. Someone who could feed them and provide a roof over their heads while they were growing up.

His mother could play many characters, and Andrew loved her dearly. Sadly for them all, "strong matriarch" wasn't in her repertoire.

She had the look of a housewife, not the strong features that Andrew, Jeff and Mercedes had inherited. They might not remember their father, but they all looked just like him.

Andrew rubbed his eyes, knowing he was beat. Right now he didn't have the energy to put up his usual denials. And besides, anyone who didn't know his mother would think him a hard-hearted Scrooge of a man for not letting his mother "live her dream."

"How much did you need?" he asked, rubbing his eyes.

"Don't you want to see what I got you?" his mother asked, trying not to look like she only came there for money.

"Oh, gee, Ma," he said, barreling through the wrapping paper. "A coffee mug. IT'S GOOD TO BE KING," he read. That was one mug that would never see the light of his office.

"I thought you'd like it," said his mother, blinking up at him innocently. How was he supposed to say no? She was his mother, after all.

With a heavy sigh, Andrew took out his checkbook and then looked at her expectantly. All he wanted right now was to get his mother out of the apartment.

"Five thou," she said, and he fought back the swear word on his tongue. Not the time, not the time, not the time. Quickly he gave her a check and then led her back to the living room.

He looked at Jamie apologetically. "She's always coming over, checking on us," he said, and his mother beamed.

Jamie looked serious, considering, like they were penned animals at the zoo. Now, Andrew knew that his family was a little off-kilter, but to be frank, whose wasn't? He wasn't sure what questions were buzzing in that too-intelligent head, but at least she was still here. And his mother was on her way out.

He helped his mother to the door and kissed her on the cheek. "I'll call you next week to see how the photographs turned out."

"Really?" she asked, eyes bright with excitement because he hated her so-called acting career and she knew it.

"Really," he promised, making a mental note to call her from the office on Tuesday. He ushered her out of the door, and then closed it behind her.

Alone, at last.

Jamie stood. "I should go," she said, dashing a gazillion hopes that had rested in his heart. However, considering his run of luck (which he now believed in), he was sure there would be some problem. A flood, erectile dysfunction (not that he'd experienced it before) or locusts descending on Broadway.

No, she was probably right.

"Can I see you home? I can call the car service."

She wrinkled her nose. "I should take a cab."

"Right," he said, fighting to keep disappointment off his face. He buzzed downstairs, and told George, the doorman, to hail a taxi. Theirs was probably the shortest after-date coupling in history. Not a proud moment. "I hope my mother didn't scare you off."

She looked at him, a question in her eyes. "She gave you a present."

"In our family, we call them bribes. Are your parents still around?"

"My father's retired military. Mom still practices. In North Dakota."

"Practices? Law?" he asked, because he could see a lawyer background in Jamie. Made perfect sense.

"Dentistry." She smiled, exposing perfect, white teeth that she normally kept hidden.

"Ah," he said, realizing there were many things he didn't know about Jamie, but he wanted to find out. She made him curious. "How did you end up on Wall Street?"

"I had excellent organizational abilities and a flair for convincing people I knew what I was doing."

"Well, that's more than most of us," he said.

"You're being modest."

"It's late, I'm tired. You've just met my mother. I had high hopes. They've been dashed. It's hard to remain a proud man. You've humbled me," he admitted.

She smiled at him and the room got a little brighter.

Right then the doorman buzzed, the signal that her cab was waiting. Andrew cursed the interruption but it seemed like tonight wasn't meant to be. However, tomorrow was another day. They rode the elevator downstairs, but he wasn't going to let her go home without resolving some very basic issues. Like when he could see her again.

"So, tomorrow. It's Saturday. You have plans other than five issues of the *Wall Street Journal?* I can summarize them all if you're interested."

She looked at him sideways. "You're very persistent."

"I like to call it focused. It's not necessarily a bad character trait. In fact," he added, "in some circumstances, focus is a good thing."

She gave him a heated look, and he felt all the carnal urges rushing back. "I remember."

The elevator door opened before he could respond and they walked outside. George, being the discreet doorman that he was, went off on his security rounds, leaving them alone. Andrew would tip him well for that.

Andrew took her in his arms and kissed her. Damn it, the cabbie could wait. Her lips opened beneath his, and he took advantage, exploring the soft confines of her mouth. Her legs parted slightly, just enough to increase the torture that he felt.

The cabbie honked, and Andrew swore.

"I should go," she said against his mouth.

"Stay," he whispered back.

Something must have clicked inside her, because she looked up, met his eyes. "I don't know if I can do this."

"What's the real issue, Jamie?" he asked, raising his head, looking into her eyes.

"I'm not impulsive. I don't do people well, and you're a man that I can't do halfway."

He wasn't sure what that meant, but it sounded like a good sign, and right now he needed all the good signs he could get. "I love the way you do people, Jamie. Just let it be. Let us be."

She looked up, blue eyes slightly muddled. "Don't make me regret this," she whispered.

"Never," he said, and took one last kiss, mainly because he needed something to live on until he saw her again. Her lips were soft, pliable, so completely unlike her, and he smiled at the inconsistent pieces.

Her arms curled tightly around his neck, and he pressed closer, feeling the trust inside her. He knew she didn't trust easily, and he wanted to reassure her. This was important to him. She was important to him, and he wanted her to know that. He wasn't great with fancy words, but he could show her. For a moment they stood on the sidewalk, lost in each other, lost in the moment. He heard the honk of the cabbie again, but this was a moment he wouldn't miss. Finally he raised his head, shook it once to clear the fog from his brain.

However, Jamie, his wonderful Jamie, was all business. She looked at him tartly. "The cab's gone."

Andrew tried not to smile, but she saw through it. "Do we need to call another one?" he asked. "It could be a long wait. Long wait. Friday night. Lots of people still out…"

In her eyes he read the answer. "Focused, huh?"

"Sometimes even devious, too," he answered. With that, he took her hand, and led her back inside.

8

FOR JAMIE, IT WAS LIKE jumping off a cliff without a parachute, golden or otherwise. They managed to get back to his apartment, a tangle of arms and mouths. Every time that rational thought filtered into her brain, Andrew banished it with a kiss or a touch of hot hands.

He backed her against the door as if he wasn't going to let her go—ever. Silly man. She wasn't going anywhere while his mouth was feasting on hers, tongues tangling. No, she wasn't going anywhere. Not now that she'd come this far.

His hands moved under her blouse, under her skirt, restless, demanding, and Jamie, never a passive one either, worked at his clothes, too. She wanted to see him, feel his skin against hers. The wait had been too long. Seven days and it seemed like forever.

A storm of emotions whirled inside her, lust, desire, passion and something else. Some nameless tenderness that she wasn't about to worry about now.

The path from the entryway to the bedroom was littered with clothes, one condom wrapper, and the remains of Jamie's sanity. For the moment she was flying high on the taste and smell of Andrew—Andrew of no last name, because sanity could be easily reclaimed with one simple reminder. He settled her on the bed, and then settled on top of her, his hard to her soft, his heat to her cold.

She looked up into his eyes, dark with that heat, darkened for her, and she was dazzled by what she saw. Slowly, forever it seemed, his mouth moved to hers, a kiss, a promise. Her heart began to race at what he was asking from her. She'd done billion-dollar deals, but never had one moment scared her so badly. Blindly, she returned his kiss, pressing her mouth against his. Tomorrow she would rationalize, plan and internalize. Tonight was all about coming alive.

"Jamie," he whispered against her lips. She pressed her face in the curve of his neck, needing to hide. Then she felt his cock against her thigh, thick and insistent, and she moaned in relief. Her legs slid open, welcoming him inside her. This she understood. He drove forward, locking them together. Then, with a hard stroke he began to move.

Again and again he thrust inside her, no hint of gentleness or reprieve, this was all about possession. With each thrust he was claiming her, marking her for his own. Her legs locked around his hips, denying him nothing. She rose to meet every rise and fall, pulling him more deeply inside her, letting her world rip apart.

Now was not the time for words, just the sound of labored breathing, the scent of his cologne and his damp skin. She needed to focus on the senses, rather than the mind. Let the hunger take over and consume her. Her fingers gripped his back, afraid of letting go, fighting against her climax. She didn't want to come back down. She didn't want sanity to return, so instead she bit her lip, welcoming the pain.

Andrew—determined, focused Andrew—would have none of it. He lifted her legs higher, pushing her to a place she'd never been before. Darkness swam around her like a cloud. She heard her own moan, a sign of weakness.

"Let go, Jamie."

"No," she argued.

"For me," he whispered.

"Please, no," she said, fighting him because she knew there was no turning back from this one simple request.

He inched her legs higher, his cock plunging in deep, and she knew she couldn't fight any longer. She felt herself fall, heard herself scream, and deep in her heart, she knew that the old Jamie McNamara would be lost forever.

ANDREW STIRRED, WANTING TO WRAP Jamie up in his arms, but she wasn't done. All that passion that lurked beneath the surface needed a place to go. Lucky for him, he was the intended recipient. Her hands rubbed over his chest, his back, his cock, never still, always finding new ways to please.

She rose over him in the moonlight, a voluptuous goddess taking him to the heights of pleasure. Her breasts shone like spun silver, full and erect. After all the fantasies he'd had, reality was so much sweeter. Jamie bent down, kissing his lips, his neck, lower still, following the trail of hair on his chest, until her lips and tongue closed around him.

He fought for a second. Tonight was supposed to be about her, but when she sucked on him, hard, he moaned, low and deep in his throat. Briskly, efficiently, she worked him over, taking him to the edge of madness. It wasn't fair. It truly wasn't fair. And as soon as his sanity returned, he would make it right. For Jamie, he would make the world a fair and just place. *For her.*

IT WAS FOUR in the morning, the time that Andrew came alive. It was his habit to eat breakfast, read the paper, watch the early morning report on MSNBC and make a task list for the day—all at the same time. He fed on his own restless energy, needing to act. Yet all he could do this morning was watch Jamie sleep. She was a restless sleeper, piling on sheets and pillows, making a mess of the duvet. Her hair fell thick and loose on her bare shoulders, her face soft, mouth slack, as if she hadn't a care in the world. She was magic.

The clock said 4:07, and he could only stare. There wasn't a to-do in the world that could drag him away from the delectable vision of watching Jamie McNamara asleep—in his bed.

The thought scared him and excited him, all at the same time. He'd never found a woman that truly understood his drive for work. For some men, it was a question of money or power. For Andrew it meant survival. When he had been young, life was simple. If he didn't work, the family wouldn't eat. Their father— godforsaken, no-account bastard, according to his mother—had left for parts unknown.

So Andrew had delivered papers, apprenticed as an electrician, and gone to school without complaint or question. It became a game to him. How far would he go? How much more could he do? Each year he pushed himself farther, and his worry about whether the family would eat became smaller and smaller. Gradually, the game was all that he was. All that he wanted to be.

Women didn't understand that. Andrew couldn't blame them. He was a self-centered, arrogant, SOB when it came right down to it. He didn't have a sensitive side, didn't have time to worry about his emotions and didn't question anything that was in his past or his future. And that was the marvelous thing about Jamie.

She understood.

She didn't think he was self-centered, or arrogant. No, Jamie saw his heart. She didn't care about having a good time or seeing the latest movie. Her drive, in business and in bed, matched his own. Magic.

He let himself watch her for another half hour, considered waking her, making love to her all over again, but he nuked that idea. Let her sleep, let her rest. There would be time soon enough. They had all weekend.

Andrew smiled at that and went into his study to work. Somehow the Fed's Report didn't seem that appealing, and instead of concentrating on quarter-point hikes, he kept remembering the seductive smell of her. For the first time in his life, Andrew Brooks was falling in love.

JAMIE'S INTERNAL CLOCK beeped at 5:30 a.m. and she kicked out of bed, blinking against the unfamiliar surroundings. Instantly her synapses powered on in her brain.

Andrew.

Oh.

Her brain stuttered for a moment, but she wouldn't let it shut down today. They had sex last night. Nothing more. They were having an affair, a torrid, sexy affair, and she didn't need to think about how successful he was, or how clients got on a list to merely talk to him, or his annual rate of return. No, she wasn't going to think about any of that.

Which didn't work at all. She fell back under the covers and pulled them over her head, trying to shut out the voices that told her she wasn't good enough, or that she'd never make it to his level.

"Shut up," she whispered to herself, smacking the voices under control. The voices obeyed.

Next, she took a deep breath, jumped out of bed, then realized she was nude, and immediately jumped back into bed.

So where was Andrew? It was 5:30 a.m. on a Saturday morning and he wasn't in bed. She gathered her clothes and got dressed. When the blouse, skirt, and shoes were neatly in place, she went to search him out.

Not that it was hard to find. The beam of a high-powered lamp led the way—to his study.

There he was, hunched over his desk, diligently reading some papers, dressed in boxers, and wearing reading glasses.

He wore reading glasses.

Her heart bumped against her ribs, loud and strong, and she was sure he was going to look up, but he didn't, so she stared, and gazed, and ogled. His hair was mussed up (she'd probably done that), and every now and then he would push his hands through it.

Still, she stood mutely, wanting the courage to speak, but afraid that the tone of her voice might give away things that she wasn't ready to give away. At least not yet.

Eventually he looked up, noticed her, and instantly the papers were put away.

"You're dressed," he said, hiding the glasses in a drawer.

"I knew you'd have things to do," she began, and then awkwardly trailed off.

He cleared his throat. "Breakfast?" •

"I don't usually eat breakfast," she answered, which sounded snippier than she meant it to, but it was the truth. Maybe a cup of coffee, but that was it.

"Oh." He padded over to stand next to her. "Do you have to leave?"

Jamie gestured toward the desk. "It looks like you have work to do."

"Habit," he said. "Does it bother you?"

She waved a hand in the air. "Not at all."

He exhaled. "Good. I didn't think you'd mind."

"No, no bother. I'll just leave you to it," she said, and turned to leave, turned away from those excellent muscles on his chest, turned away from the little dimple on the left side of his cheek…

He caught her hand. "I don't have to work," he said, and pulled her to him. Pulled her closer to the excellent muscles on his chest. Close enough to spy the little dimple on the left side of his cheek. Her blood pumped twice.

"You don't?" she asked weakly.

His hands, knowing all the shortcuts, cut underneath her blouse, kneading her back. His mouth found the one exact spot on her neck that was guaranteed to melt her spine.

"Maybe for just a little bit," she answered. With that, he lifted her in his arms and carried her back to bed.

NOON CAME WAY TOO EARLY for Andrew. He'd never understood the appeal of lying in bed on a lazy Saturday morning—until this very moment.

"So this is why people sleep late?" he asked, while nuzzling Jamie's belly button.

She stretched lazily, muscles tightening. "It would certainly explain much. I think I need to go back to my apartment."

He raised his head. Glared. "I think that's a miserable idea."

"I need clothes," she muttered.

He continued exploring the smooth white skin of her stomach. "No, you don't."

"I'm not comfortable nude. It's very—bare. At some point in time, I will need clothes."

"We can go shopping."

Jamie rolled her eyes. "We don't need to shop. Seriously. It's very nice of you to offer, but save your money. Besides, I only shop the sales. Too expensive otherwise."

"You don't like to shop?" he asked, not quite sure if he believed her. All women liked to shop. It was genetic.

"Oh, I do like to shop, but you have to keep an eye out for the bargains. It's like a hunt. Finding the best deals. You need a list and a plan."

His heart flipped over twice in his chest.

"We can hit your place later," he said, because right now he had a plan of his own.

"It's getting really late…" she started, but then his lips trailed further down her belly, finding the tight, damp curls between her thighs. He knew how to end this argument. He took her in his mouth and suckled— hard. Sure enough, Jamie gave up the fight.

AT THREE IN THE AFTERNOON, Jamie won. Metaphorically speaking of course, since she'd already taken home the gold several times. The physical sating kept her in that emotional nirvana where she didn't have to worry about anything beyond the next orgasm. It wasn't a bad life. Truly.

All she had to do was focus on the physical-ness of their relationship. But the personal questions bubbled up inside her, like hemlock, and she wasn't used to holding her tongue. Eventually she had to know the one thing that kept her fascinated.

"Have you always been like this?" she asked, pulling up the sheets discreetly.

"Insatiable? No. That's recent," he answered.

Jamie felt a hot blush run up her cheeks, and she wasn't by nature a blusher. "I meant the work." She gestured to the pile of magazines and newspapers stacked neatly alongside his bed.

He considered them seriously. "Yeah, pretty much. What about you?"

"I like to work," she said, because she did like to work, but more than that. She needed to work. As the oldest child of two overachievers, her parents had pushed her to excel. But they didn't have to push hard, her genes had hardwired it in her.

Work fed Jamie's confidence and fed her strength. As the stakes in her job went higher, when the deals became more complicated, and the clients became more demanding, she needed the confidence more than ever. When it came to money and finance, men sensed weakness like sharks to blood. She'd seen the downfall of more than one female in the industry.

All because they lost the edge.

"That's good then," he answered, then dove back beneath the covers. However, Jamie wasn't quite ready to abandon the issue. "Do you have a lot of friends?"

"No," he said, his voice muffled, his fingers walking their way up her thigh.

"Why not?" she asked, and then gasped as he started a more personal exploration.

"Never thought about it much," he said, his fingers circling inside her. Her hips arched and rocked, and her eyes fluttered closed. It was too hard to think. He made it so hard for her to think. Her head fell back against the pillows and she gave herself up to him once more.

LATER THAT AFTERNOON, they finally got to her building, because Jamie truly *did* need clothes. She wasn't a "wear your clothes twice" sort of girl, because her mother had conditioned her to the whole torn-under-wear-car accident connection. As they walked into the lobby, Stephanie was heading out. Stephanie did a not-so-discreet double take while Jamie discreetly glared.

Stephanie received the message, but then changed course and moved behind Andrew, waiting with them for the elevator. Jamie took a step back as well. Just in case.

First Stephanie pointed meaningfully at Andrew's back, a question in her eyes.

Jamie gave her a quick nod.

Then Stephanie cupped her hands behind Andrew's butt while gaping in an approving manner.

Jamie made a quick cutting motion against her throat, until Stephanie shot her an A-OK sign with her thumb and forefinger.

The elevator dinged, and the three of them got on, Stephanie once again taking the rear position.

"We should go get something to eat. Do you like Indian?" asked Andrew.

Out of the corner of her eye, Jamie saw Stephanie fanning herself, but she ignored Steph and smiled at Andrew tightly. "I love Indian. There's a great place around the corner."

"Or a movie? Maybe we should do a movie. God, I haven't been out in ages. What do normal people do?"

Behind him, Stephanie shook her head negatively, sliding her hips in a move mainly seen in pole dancing contests.

Jamie covered her face.

"You don't like movies?" asked Andrew.

She gave him a radiant smile. "Whatever you decide."

At that, Stephanie pantomimed an obscene gesture, and Jamie struggled to maintain her last semblance of composure.

"I'm not supposed to be seeing any of this, am I," Andrew said to no one in particular.

Thankfully, right then the elevator dinged, and Stephanie stepped out, giving Jamie and Andrew a huge wave. She would pay later. An extra thirty minutes or the treadmill, or possibly forfeit her life.

But right now, Jamie wanted to sink into the floor.

"Friend of yours?" he asked.

"Mental patient," answered Jamie. "Just ignore her, she does that to all the residents."

JAMIE AND ANDREW SPENT Sunday together, first arguing over the automotive forecast in the *Wall Street Journal* and then heckling the guests on Meet the Press. Andrew's mind was sharp, sharper than Jamie's, which was saying something, and not something she said often. She liked to watch him think, liked to watch the way his eyes would narrow in concentration as he mulled over his words. He wasn't impulsive with his speech like she was, and she loved debating with him, loved the arguments, because then they could make up. And as good a debater as he was, he was even better at making up. First in the shower, then on the kitchen table, and when they debated the world's energy crisis in his study, she admitted defeat when he backed her against his desk, and slid off her shorts and undies. Not content with a mere victory of mind, he bent before her, his eyes dark and wicked, and lowered his head between her legs. Then his tongue demonstrated to her in glorious detail that there were alternative ways of drilling for oil, it just took a little ingenuity.

Jamie was convinced.

Yet all good things must come to an end. And when Sunday evening arrived, Jamie knew that the blissful weekend was over. It was time to go back to the Real World.

Andrew was flying out to L.A. for a couple of days, and Jamie had clients of her own to think about. Like Newhouse, for instance.

She thought about asking Andrew's advice, knew that this was a remarkable opportunity to learn something from him, but she couldn't bring herself to do it. Not because he wouldn't help, oh, no, she knew he would. But because if he gave her stellar advice, which of course, he would, and she followed through, which of course, she would, and the deal came through, then she could no longer claim the success as her own. Suddenly she was riding on someone else's coattails. There were people in the world who rode on coattails, but not Jamie. Nope, not Jamie.

So on Sunday night she left his apartment, leaving behind a toothbrush and a set of sweats, things she'd never done with Todd, things she never even thought about doing with Todd. But she'd never felt this shock of emotion before, and best of all, Andrew actually looked pleased.

As she took the subway back to her apartment, she took the opportunity to work on a fool-proof plan for Newhouse. Quietly she exorcised the giddy teenager from her consciousness, focusing her thoughts back on work. Wall Street wasn't a place for giddiness or fits of giggles or teenagers.

When she finally arrived at her apartment, she pulled her hair back into a tight ponytail, locked herself in front of her computer, downed two cans of Red Bull and got serious.

It took some hours, some fresh thinking, some clever research techniques and two more cans of Red Bull, but by 3:00 a.m., she had developed a ten-pronged attack. On Monday, she had a late afternoon meeting with a telecommunications client in Dallas, but by the following morning, she would be ready to execute.

ANDREW IGNORED HIS promise to Old Lady Feldman until Monday night, when he happened to hear another knock, a sound he was learning to recognize as the door knocker for 43C. Now, he knew Jamie was in Dallas, so it couldn't be her, and his enthusiasm for the outside world waned. However, he'd said he'd take care of things, and Andrew prided himself on taking care of things. Other people made promises. Andrew didn't make many promises, he just delivered.

So Andrew got up, opened his door, and peeked out in the hallway, pretending he was checking for a pizza delivery. This time the man was an older guy, late fifties maybe, with the shifty eyes of a man ashamed of what he's doing. Working on Wall Street, Andrew had seen the type. Andrew glanced his way and grimaced. "Sorry. Thought you were the pizza guy. Guess I'm really hungry," he said, sounding just like an idiot. He'd never been a good liar like Jeff was.

The shifty-eyed man looked down at the carpet. "Sorry. No pizza here."

"Nope," said Andrew, deciding to do a little investigative work. "Hey, listen, I had some men's shirts that disappeared from my laundry delivery and I think they might have gotten delivered somewhere else by mistake. She have a husband or boyfriend or brother or something that lives with her?"

The man looked at Andrew weirdly. "No."

However, since the Rhinestone Queen in 43C hadn't answered the door yet, he decided to continue. "Hey, look. I made that up. Sorry. See, we've had some break-ins in the area, and I'm part of the building's safety committee and as part of that, we keep an eye out for suspicious characters, not that I'm saying you're a suspicious character, but you can see why I would want to check?"

The man looked worried, his gray brows arrowing together. "Break-ins? Really? I should tell Stella."

Stella? The Rhinestone Queen was called Stella. It seemed fitting somehow.

"You see Stella often?" asked Andrew, bracing a shoulder against his doorway, being the nosy yet sociable neighbor.

"An hour once a week. Wednesday night's my slot," he answered, and then the mysterious Stella opened the door, wearing a long pink robe trimmed in, yes, rhinestones.

"Terry! Come in," she said, and then she spied Andrew in the hallway. "Good evening," she told him, and it still didn't sound like a proposition, which both relieved and disappointed Andrew all at the same time.

"Night," he answered. "Keep those doors locked," he said, mainly for good measure.

After he was back in his apartment, Andrew considered the evidence. She saw men in one-hour slots. Only men. Never women. And her name was Stella and she wore rhinestones. Ergo, laws were being broken. Moral codes were being violated, and the property values of the building would plummet once the scandal was exposed.

Andrew frowned to himself.

He needed to figure out a way to stop her, or even better, have her kicked out of the building. His frown turned to a grim smile as he opened his PDA, because he knew the perfect man for the job.

THE HEADQUARTERS OF Newhouse International was a nondescript two-story sprawl of a building in Stamford. The grounds were green and covered with cool flowers that probably took gee-gobs of money and time to maintain. Completely impractical. Gorgeous, yet expensive, and impractical. Jamie shook her head and walked inside, handing the security guard her business card.

"I'm here to see Sandy Arenson," she stated and then smiled politely.

The guard picked up his phone and Jamie waited breathlessly, hoping the Gorgon was in a cheery mood. She needed a break with Newhouse. She deserved a break. She deserved this break.

Miraculously, the Gorgon's weekend must have been as great as Jamie's, because Jamie was buzzed up into the inner sanctum. At last.

And about time.

Once she got upstairs, she immediately saw the difference between Wall Street and software companies. The place was a forest of cubicles, with only three offices in the far corner. There were whiteboards everywhere, airplanes hanging from the ceiling, and huge dual monitors that Jamie, who had never been a technoid, actually lusted after.

Manning the front of one of the offices was a mild-mannered woman with blue-tinted John Lennon glasses.

The Gorgon.

And yet—not so Gorgonly. Jamie advanced, preparing for battle. "Sandy, thank you for buzzing me up. I was in the neighborhood and I felt so bad about the missed meeting that I knew I had to do something nice." She pulled out a wicker basket. "Do you like cheese? I had heard…"

The eyes behind blue lenses widened and Jamie knew she had struck gold. Cheese gold. Her source— a classmate of Sanji's who was interning at Newhouse—was right.

"How did you know?" asked Sandy, offering Jamie a chair.

Jamie took it, plopped down, and laid the offering on Sandy's desk. "I make it my business to find out what I can about my clients."

Unable to resist, the secretary took a slice of the gouda and immediately made ambrosia-face. "This is marvelous. Murray's?"

Jamie shook her head. "Actually, there's a better place on the East Side. We'll have to do a jaunt there sometime."

Sandy put another slice in her mouth. "Heaven." Then she put aside the basket. "I have to put this away," she said, clearing the desk, exposing the morning's *Wall Street Journal.*

Jamie took the opening and ran with it. "Sandy, you know that Bond-Worthington is anxious to show Mr. Newhouse exactly what we can do for him. I believe it's a win-win. I have a sample portfolio that we designed specifically for his holdings. Goldman is doing him no favors by investing so heavily in Asia-Pac."

The not-so-much-a-Gorgon nodded in agreement, still eyeing the basket.

"I'd like to get on Mr. Newhouse's calendar. Even half an hour would go a long way toward convincing him that we're the best game in town for him."

Sandy held up her hand, stopping Jamie mid-spiel. "You convinced me already. Let me go talk to Arnie," she said with a wink. "He listens to me."

She got up and departed behind closed doors, leaving Jamie alone to skim over the *WSJ*. There was a red sticky flag attached to one of the pages and Jamie flipped it open to see exactly what was on Newhouse's radar. And there he was. Andrew Brooks. Her Andrew Brooks. *Wall Street Wunderkind. Beating the Dow, one Hedge at a Time.*

It wasn't a great picture. Nice enough, but they hadn't captured the way his eyes lit up when he started talking about the market, or the way he was always moving, restless, his eyes looking on the horizon, new places to go, new bets to make. The article was almost reverential. She could have been happy with everything, except for the yellow sticky note, and the scribbled handwriting: "Get me a meeting!"

Jamie closed the paper on the serious dark eyes, and sat back in her chair.

Newhouse wanted Andrew. Because, of course, Andrew was the best. Not Jamie's firm. *Andrew.*

She clamped her heels together, and sat up straight.

It didn't make her feel better, but she knew good posture made people think you felt great. Perky. Confident.

Not like a bird flying blind into the great, glass windows that graced Wall Street. Sandy returned and Jamie shook off the sting. The pain would return in a bit, but this was business.

Always business.

"He'll see you on Friday, lunch," she said, snagging an extra bite of aged cheddar. "Mmm… This is so delicious. We'll definitely do that trip," said the Gorgon, happily munching away.

Jamie picked up her bag and waved at her new best friend. It was just business, she kept repeating in her mind, and by the time the train had returned to Grand Central, she almost believed it herself.

9

THE NEXT MORNING, Andrew called. Just to talk. Jamie didn't feel much like talking yet. Her pride stung, but she couldn't tell him that. She would be number one jerkette extraordinaire if she told him that.

She spent a few minutes pouring over the last ten years of financials from Newhouse International, gathering her ammunition for the presentation.

Unfortunately, her gaze kept coming back to rest on the *Wall Street Journal* profile.

The one man who could make her forget herself, and he was King Midas in the hedge fund community. They were the gamblers and gunslingers who traded outside the laws of the SEC, men who lived and died by their bets. And dagnabbit, they were the one community that had made returns hand over fist for the past four years.

It all seemed so unfair. She could list the reasons why this would be a bad idea, but it would take two hands and both feet as well. First, he was not a peer. In the hierarchy, he sat several levels above her—Mt. Olympus levels. Second, the rules he worked by were "old school, old boys, old Scotch." Jamie had spent the last eight years being oppressed by those rules. Her list of deficiencies was long: never went to Yale, not a boy, old or otherwise, and threw up at the taste of Scotch. No, she couldn't even begin to compete. All that was left was earning her stripes the old-fashioned way. One razor-sharp stiletto at a time.

And then there was his family. The Brooks family seemed communicative. Affectionate. They even gave presents.

She picked up the phone, speed-dialed her mom, and then listened as said maternal unit began to recite the current health status of the entire McNamara clan. Finally, Jamie broke in.

"Mom, can I ask you a question?"

"Of course. Curiosity is a sign of an active mind. Questions should to be encouraged."

"Why didn't you ever give me a present?"

"Jamie, you got presents every year, twice a year. You've forgotten to take your Vitamin A, haven't you? And add more fish to your diet. Keeps the mind sharp."

Sometimes Jamie wondered if she shouldn't be more screwed up then she was. She heaved a sigh. "Besides Christmas, besides my birthday. Why didn't you ever give me a present for no apparent reason?" If Andrew's mother could give him a coffee mug on a Friday night—just because—it seemed like there was something that Jamie might be missing out on.

"I don't know, Jamie. Your father and I thought that

too much arbitrary gifting would turn you more materialistic, and we didn't want to encourage that."

"But you didn't give me any arbitrary gifts, and I'm terribly materialistic. I like things, Mom. Possessions. Luxuries. iPods. I own thirty-seven pairs of shoes. That's materialistic."

Her mother heaved a sigh this time. "Your sister is not materialistic at all, so obviously it worked for her. You were always a unique child, Jamie. Very set in your ways, and I'm not sure we could have done anything to fix that."

Jamie wasn't sure she liked the idea of being "fixed," but her mother's people skills ranked right up there with her own, so she gave her mother a pass. "All right. I'm thinking of coming down for a weekend, maybe Easter or something."

"Whatever you decide to do is fine by us. The spare bedroom is available, although Rose and the grandkids will be here. That reminds me, I need to pick up the new Playstation game for Trevor. He's such a little cutie-pie."

"You give Rose's kids presents when they visit?" asked Jamie, thinking she was an awful person for being jealous of her own nieces and nephews. What did that say about her sensitivity chip? It was absent. That's what it said. "Listen, I need to go. I have Pilates in an hour. Give Dad a hug." She hesitated for a moment. "I miss you, Mom."

Her mother was silent. "I miss you, too, Jamie. Call next week. On Saturday the rates are low."

Jamie hung up, trying not to dwell on the dynamics, or lack thereof, of her family. Instead, she licked her own wounds, grateful to be flying out to Atlanta for the day.

JFK was not the most elegant airport in the world. There was always construction, always traffic, and always mile-long lines to get through security. Jamie picked up her boarding pass, and was just ready to brave the TSA minions when she heard her name.

Immediately she recognized the voice, as did every nerve ending in her body. "Andrew?"

And there he was. Dark hair. Dark suit. Conservatively refined blue tie with a Windsor knot. Her heart sighed. "Why are you here?"

He held up a brown Macy's bag. "Present."

"Really?" she said, happiness warring with pride, and happiness winning out. It wasn't his fault he was a genius when it came to predicting the market. It wasn't his fault that his company made everyone else look like schlubs.

And he brought her a present.

He shrugged, one lock of hair falling on his forehead. "You know, just something for the trip."

A present. Jamie fought the urge to grin. Instead, she opened up the bag and pulled out—

A bottle of water.

"Fancy," she said, smiling.

"Planes. Dehydration. If you don't fly in business class or better, they never give you enough water. I always pack an extra in the backpack."

"Fancy, yet practical as well."

"There's more."

She reached inside and pulled out—a Starbucks cup.

"Grande mocha latte, nonfat," he recited.

"You know that?" she asked, completely impressed, and trying desperately not to show it.

"Research is my business."

"But if I drink this, the caffeine cancels out the water," she said, needing to correct him, simply because she was that way.

"I wanted to cover all the bases. You might not be a plane-water drinker, but a plane-coffee drinker."

"Very ingenious."

"There's more."

She reached inside and pulled out—*Cosmo.*

She raised her eyebrows. *"Cosmo?"*

He opened the bag and pulled out another magazine. *"Business Week,* too."

"I'm beginning to sense a trend," she said, not really caring what was shining in her eyes. There was one guaranteed way to Jamie's heart—idiotic presents.

"A positive or negative trend?"

"The most positives of positives."

"There's more."

Next she pulled out a Powerbar. "Okay, this one I get." She dug in the bag. "No candy bar?"

He reached into his pocket. "Hershey bar."

"Oh, for this I will love you forever."

"Well, they're only eighty-nine cents at the newsstand."

"What can I say, my heart is cheap."

"And there's one more thing."

She reached inside and pulled out—a single red rose. "Oh."

"I didn't know if you liked roses or not."

"What? No orchids," she asked, wanting to make a joke, wanting to do something to pull air into her lungs.

"No orchids. Just a rose." This time there was no hesitation, no doubt in his voice.

Her lips curved upward, a tiny smile that indicated nothing of the full-scale orchestra that was playing inside her. "I'll keep it under my pillow tonight."

He took her hand in his. "I was thinking about you. Just wanted to see you again. We'll talk more when you get back, Jamie."

Oh, he really didn't fight fair. Jamie closed her eyes, because she was more than halfway in love with him, and each time he said her name with that catch in his voice, each time he stroked her skin, his place in her heart grew larger and larger.

His lips met hers and then pulled away. "Dream of me, Jamie."

She gazed up into dark brown eyes that held her captive in ways she'd never thought possible. She didn't know what to say, didn't know what to do, only knew that he represented everything she'd always fought against, every promotion that'd been given to a Y chromosome less deserving than her. It didn't seem fair that a mere man could slip beneath her defenses so easily.

"I'll see you tomorrow."

"I have lunch with a client," she said, not quite a lie, and not the truth.

"Dinner, then."

"What about Friday?" asked Jamie, still needing to keep some of the walls between them.

Andrew didn't look happy, but he nodded. "Friday."

Then the announcer called her flight and she took a step back.

"My plane," she said stupidly and then went to stand in line.

Before she went through the metal detector, she turned and saw him standing there, watching. She'd never had a man ask so much of her, without asking for anything at all. Andrew Brooks scared the hell out of her. Her mind might have poised to run, but her heart wasn't about to walk away. Presents did that to her.

LATE THAT SAME DAY, only ten minutes from the closing bell, Jeff showed up at Andrew's office. Whenever Jeff showed up at his office, it meant trouble. Sometimes family issues, mostly women. Jeff liked to whine a lot, but Andrew suspected he just liked to talk, which was why Andrew approved of Jeff's career choice. PR was the perfect outlet for Jeff's need to spin the truth for fun and profit.

"Why are you here?" he asked, not looking up from the terminal. The timing of the buy-order was critical, and the window of opportunity was closing fast. Andrew watched the digits increase, one slow fraction at a time.

"I need you to go to a party with me."

Andrew's eyes never left the slowing increasing prices. "Another pretend bachelor party?"

Jeff didn't even bother with pretend guilt. "No. This one is for *M* magazine. I'm supposed to be there watching over our new client."

"And you need my help for this?"

"Mercedes can't go. And even if she said yes, she's not the most reliable."

"Glad to be wanted, but no. Ask a regular date. You know I don't like those things," he complained, secretly pleased that he was actually being considered for social functions that didn't involve strippers. Maybe his brother was moving up in the world.

"I'm supposed to take a client to the party, so I can't very well bring a date."

"You want me to come along? And what twisted reasoning is behind this idea?"

"It's Sheldon Summerville," said Jeff, as if that explained all.

"Who?" asked Andrew, mildly annoyed that Entergy had ticked up another three-eighths of a point; he'd shorted it last week.

"The socialite. Daughter of consumer product tycoon, Wayne Summerville. Of Summerville Consumer Products. They're our newest client. Her dad wants me to improve her image."

"Congratulations," said Andrew automatically, still watching the ticker.

"She's a pain in the ass. Her father wants everything perfect, everything scripted, but wouldn't you know it?

The woman is a lush. Get her within a mile of alcohol and she starts firing her mouth off to anyone in pants."

"Sounds like most of your dates."

"Her father's a client," he answered back.

"Ah, said bodacious behavior is all right for women you date, but not women you have to represent."

"It makes my job hell."

Andrew looked up again, studying his brother. "Is that maturity rearing its ugly head? Nah. Couldn't be."

"Will you come with me?"

"No," said Andrew happily.

"I need the babysitting help."

"How old is she? Ten?"

"Twenty-five. A very *young* twenty-five."

"My brother, the babysitter. When is it?" asked Andrew, pretending he might go.

"It's Friday. Eight o'clock."

Imagine that. He didn't even have to lie. "Sorry, bro. Got plans."

"Change them. The market's closed. Nothing important happens after the bell rings."

"It's not work," said Andrew, finally seeing the in he wanted. He jumped on ten thousand shares, counted his profit, and sighed. "It's a good day when a man can rack up a cool mill for his fund."

Jeff didn't even look impressed. "You have to go. I'll pay you."

Andrew looked up and scanned his brother's face, surprised at the urgency there. It only made rejection sweeter. "I have a date," answered Andrew, deciding the best way out was to tell the truth. Jeff wouldn't believe anything else. Sad.

"Oh? The Hummer chick? Man, bring her along. It'd be perfect!"

"To meet my brother, who outted our personal affairs to the entire financial community? Do I look stupid?"

"Oh, come on. How long are you going to keep her in the closet? Mom told me about her. Did you get laid, preferably in another moving vehicle?" asked Jeff, as if discussing sexual affairs with their mother was a normal occurrence.

"If you think I'm going to tell you anything else, you've been playing in the mercury again."

"You did!" Jeff slapped the desk. "God, this is serious."

Andrew saw himself neatly trapped. His pride wouldn't let him admit he didn't get laid, but his loyalty to Jamie wouldn't let him lie, either. "Leave her alone."

"Bring her to the party. Think of it, a chance to meet the rest of the family. I swear I'll be on my best behavior," he said, crossing his chest.

"No."

"You're such a dirtbag, Andrew."

"Yes, I am. Now leave."

"You haven't read the latest, have you?"

And even the pleasure of a cool million dimmed at that. "What do you mean?"

"Jack and Honey." Jeff made obscene finger gestures. Andrew got the point.

"I don't want to know," he said, using denial as a shield. "It's someone else's personal life now."

"Well, yeah, but she's got you down."

"I thought she was going to write fiction."

"The best fiction is based on reality. I thought you told her she could?"

Something red and dangerous flared in Andrew's vision. "That's what she told you? I talked it over with Jamie and we decided against it. What did she say this time?"

Jeff laughed like the devil he was and handed over the paper. "I printed out a copy," he said.

Andrew buried his face in his hands. "Why didn't she pick you?"

"I didn't have sex in a Hummer, Andrew. Although now I'm honestly thinking about it. You've got some pretty big—uh, shoes—to fill."

"You're jealous of this, aren't you?" said Andrew, finally realizing the absolute depths of his brother's fascination with all things sexual.

Jeff shook his head. "You threw me a curveball. I admit. Limos, toys, next thing I know, you'll be buying her nipple rings. I used to think I could keep up, but—" He grinned, "you're doing such a balls-out great job. Makes me proud."

Andrew threw the *Times* at his brother, who took the hint. "Leave. I'll have you thrown out."

Jeff didn't buy it.

"I mean it," said Andrew, picking up the receiver.

Finally Jeff looked beat. "All right. Not feeling the

love here, so I'll go. But definitely read that, and then see if maybe you should take her to the party after all," he said, closing the door behind him.

Andrew picked up the paper and began to read

Jack and Honey have certainly outted themselves, going from demure and sedate to an all-out public-offering pleasure fest at a star-studded party this weekend. It started out innocuous enough, the requisite dirty dancing on the dance floor, but not even his usually austere nature could hide Jack's capital assets. Then the couple moved to the privacy of the VIP room where a booth was reserved for um, more private transactions.

Her skirt's fabric to flesh ratio ran as weak as the dollar, and many witnesses indicated au naturel was the undergarment of choice, causing a flutter of irrational exuberance for all. The bouncer was given a hearty tip to ensure that the couple got the privacy they desired, but canoodling couples beware! The Red Choo Diaries have spies everywhere. Before dinner (he was having the clam dip), our Honey spent the time with her head arched back, her lips pursed in a perfect O. The breasts thrust against her shirt, nipples jauntily peaked as Jack took her to Dow ten thousand again and again. However, the moral of this story, or immorality, depending on your jaundiced viewpoint, is that one good fingering deserves another, and outperforming Honey didn't hesitate to put her mouth where his money was.

Jack, usually a very dull boy, found himself riding a bull market punctuated by a vocabulary not seen since Black Monday in '87. All in all, it was a night of after-hours trading to be seen, and of course, discussed in detail for weeks. At least until Jack and Honey decide to entertain us again.

IT TOOK HIM LESS than thirty minutes to make it down to Mercedes's apartment. "How could you do it?" he asked, and then noticed his mother sitting on her couch.

Andrew began to wonder if he was cursed, or if all families operated the way his did.

"What?" asked his sister, all innocence.

Andrew looked at his mother, then back at Mercedes. "You know."

"You told me I could."

"I was trying to be nice, Mercedes. I didn't think you would actually do it. I thought you were going to use someone else," he said, lowering his voice.

"I was. But then this agent called. And she loves my stuff, and she *loves* the exploits of Honey and Jack. She thinks it'd make a great book."

"No."

"Who're Honey and Jack?" asked Thea.

"They're people from work," he answered quickly.

"I wish you'd introduce me to more of your friends, Andrew. That Jamie seemed very personable. Maybe a little stodgy. I wish you'd find some nice girl who could cook."

"I like Jamie," he said, needing to defend her, because he was pretty sure she didn't cook.

His mother patted his arm. "And it's a good thing that you do. You work too much. You need a social life."

Mercedes preened. "She's right, Andrew. Lighten up. Live a little."

Not wanting to hear a critique of his social life, or lack thereof, Andrew changed the subject. "How did the audition go?" he asked Thea.

Her face fell. It was one of the main reasons that Andrew hated his mother's desire to be an actress. The rejections—and there were lots—were hell on her. "There'll be others," she answered.

"So why do you worry about working anyway? Relax. Retire."

"Andrew, I need this. I need to do something on my own. You do everything for me. You just let an old woman worry about her own life for once."

"You're not old," he said, not committing to the rest. He would always take care of her, always protect her, always make sure that she didn't have any problems in her life. That's what Andrew did for the people he loved. "What did your agent say?"

"I fired him," she said, and Andrew looked at her, surprised, yet pleased.

"Really?"

Thea looked down, studied the carpet. "I think he

was just after my money. Always expenses for this, expenses for that."

"I'm proud of you, Ma."

"Are you going to look for another agent?" asked Mercedes. "I know some people."

His mother waved a hand. "Your people are all book people. I need movie people. Lou Steinman is supposed to be excellent, but I'm probably not good enough for him…" she said.

Steinman? Andrew filed the name away in his head. "Of course you are, Ma. Why don't you go home? I need to talk to Mercedes."

Mercedes looked alarmed. "Let her stay. I don't get to see my mother enough," she said, coming to stand in front of Thea.

"I'll stay," announced his mother, and Andrew resigned himself to the fact that his family would never, ever play fair.

"Fine," he said, and lapsed into a coughing fit.

Instantly Thea was at his side. "Are you okay?"

"Water," he said weakly.

And like the good mother she was, Thea was off to the kitchen.

Andrew turned on Mercedes. "You're not doing a book."

"What if they already offered?" she answered, her jaw jutting in the war position.

"I don't care. I will not have Jamie put through this."

"Oh, yeah. Poor Jamie. Like this isn't completely about you."

"What does that mean?"

"Come on, Andrew. Anything that gets in the way of that pedestal you're standing on gets annihilated."

"Mercedes, this is not about me. It's about the personal lives of two people that you have no business writing about. This has to stop."

"It's my big chance. Besides, it's fiction."

"Now it is. But what happens if names get attached? They're already buzzing around the brokerage houses, trying to figure out who's Honey and who's Jack. It's only a matter of time."

"And wouldn't that be rough. If Jack got outted…"

"Yes, it would be. Take the stories down."

"I'm not."

"You will. Somebody could get hurt."

"Yeah, like me. You don't understand, Andrew. I've got two publishers courting me directly, and I think William Morris is going to make an offer of representation. I can't just change horses in midstream."

"Find a new horse, Mercedes."

"I'll lose everything," she muttered, besides Mercedes never had enough faith in herself.

"If you're good, it won't matter."

"You don't think I'm good enough, do you?"

"Getting in print is hard. If that's what you're serious about doing, let me talk to a few people."

"Forget it. I'll do it on my own."

"I'm trying to help."

"Leave my career alone."

"Leave my life alone."

Just then, Thea returned with a glass of water. "Here you are, dear. Drink up."

Andrew took the glass and downed it, casting a long glance at Mercedes. He only hoped he could trust her.

WHEN JAMIE READ the entry in the Red Choo Diaries, she was almost relieved. Here, written in twelve point font, was a clear-cut reason to be mad at Andrew.

It was much easier to make him a cad than a wonderful, hard-working man who just happened to be better than she was. Unfortunately, that little lie lasted about three minutes. She climbed into bed that night, staring up at her ceiling, wondering what else she could do to make herself more successful. What ten-step plan could she devise that would bring her to his level of ability? She'd been taught that with hard work and sacrifice, she could achieve anything. That she could do anything. That she could be better than anyone. Was that just another lie in an unjust world?

"We're number two," might work as an ad for a car commercial, but it was no way to live a life.

The worries lasted until he called her to apologize for his sister's latest. Jamie laughed it off. Exposing sexual secrets to the world was small change compared to exposing weakness in herself.

She didn't know if he sensed the war inside her and she wasn't about to tell him. It seemed silly when she voiced it aloud, even to herself.

For thirty minutes they talked about nothing in particular. He had a special talent with her. Normally she hated to talk about nothing. With Andrew, nothing became everything.

Every time she talked to him, every time she saw him, every time she thought of him, she got sucked in deeper and deeper, and she pushed the worries further and further away.

The next morning she found Stephanie at the gym, pedaling away on the stationary bike, which immediately cheered her up because Stephanie was a wonderful salve to a beaten ego. If Stephanie went fast, Jamie could go faster. If Stephanie contorted herself into a pretzel, Jamie could bend better. It might have been stupid, she knew it was stupid, but being number two really sucked.

However, as a sad commentary on her current situation, today Steph was out-pedaling her.

Somewhere, somehow, God was laughing, pointing a long, God-like finger at her and in general telling her that she'd never be number one at anything.

Eventually Jamie collapsed, winded and beaten. "Who are you and what have you done with Stephanie?"

Stephanie's evil twin flashed her a wide smile. "I, my sloth-like friend, have lost seven pounds, owing to a low-carb, low-sugar, low-food, all water and grapefruit diet, and I am pumped," she said, ending with one fist waving in the air.

Jamie, who hadn't lost a pound, merely glared. "Don't go all movie star on me, missy."

"You are such a spoilsport, Jamester. Why the unusually melancholy mien, even more so than the norm?"

Jamie sighed and climbed up on the treadmill. "Do you ever feel lost, Steph?" Which wasn't exactly "I'm jealous of my boyfriend," but it was close.

Stephanie climbed up and started ramping up the speed and incline. "Only in Brooklyn. That place just messes with my head, you know?"

"I don't mean lost in the geographic sense, I mean, lost in the 'why am I suddenly hearing voices?' sense?"

Steph looked nervous. "Have you seen a doctor about this? They have programs…"

Jamie sighed again. If she was going to feel sorry for herself, she might as well do it right. "I've always been focused on achieving my goals, balancing my 401K at year-end, keeping on budget, analyzing my career plan to see where I was headed, and I was always on track. Always," she said, bumping down the resistance.

"You really do all that crap? Jeez, Jamie, they only tell you that in books to make you feel guilty when you *don't* do it. It's a huge marketing scam. You didn't know that?"

Jamie stopped, the treadmill still going, then realized she couldn't stop, she had to keep moving. A solitary rat caught in the cog. "It always worked before."

"I think I must hate you, then. Although you're lucky, I've lost poundage. Not feeling the hate."

"I'm serious, Steph."

"So was I," answered Stephanie. "Okay, so tell me about the voices? What's got your tennies so tied up?"

"I'll never be number one. He's always going to be better," she said, her voice almost a whisper.

"He? Why didn't I guess this was about a man? *The* man?"

"Andrew."

"Hunky studo-rama. He's number one? And I suppose we're talking business, not, like grilling steaks, or some other manly pursuit?"

"He made the cover of *Forbes,*" muttered Jamie.

"No kidding," said Steph, awe in her voice.

"You're not helping."

Immediately Steph erased the awe from her face. "Sorry. That really sucks."

"It shouldn't suck. Every woman in America would be over the moon if her boyfriend made the cover of *Forbes,* or is quoted weekly in the *Wall Street Journal,* or if he makes more money than the Rockefellers."

"He's rich? Oh, man, Jamie. You didn't tell me that."

"You're still not helping."

"Why is this a problem?"

"I don't know," Jamie answered, even though she did.

"You are not communicating. Practice your words."

"Why can't he be normal? Or at least average?"

"You want average? There're fifty thousand pudgy bachelors in Queens that are just dying to meet a woman like you."

"Queens? You've got to be kidding."

"I rest my case."

"What case?" asked Jamie, slumping over the handles of the treadmill. Bad posture be damned.

"You will never be normal. You will never be average. You will never fall in love with average, nor normal. Accept it, be done with it, and tell the voices to shut up."

"I didn't say I was in love," said Jamie, fear rising inside her.

Steph shot her an evil grin and pumped up the speed on the treadmill, preparing to beat Jamie in a clash of the not-so-much-Titans. Jamie matched the speed and ran like her heart depended on it. She had a feeling that it did.

ANDREW MET BOONE SLAGER at Fizz for drinks. He didn't usually meet Boone for drinks, but then, he usually didn't try to get someone kicked out of a building, either. For that, alcohol in an overpriced gin joint seemed appropriate.

Fizz was a dark place with polished wood floors, comfortable leather chairs and the discreet lighting that was favored by most Wall Street types when doing business of a seedier nature.

Boone had been at Yale two years ahead of Andrew, but he had stayed in touch, mainly because Andrew had money now. Over the years, Andrew had realized that having friends with money was pretty important to most Yale graduates.

"Boone, got a favor."

Boone, who didn't get a chance to do favors for Andrew often, perked up, eyes sparkling in the dark light. "Anything, my man."

"You're the head of the building's board. It's about 43C." Then Andrew made a face. It was the subjective, judgmental face seen on thousands of New Yorkers every day. You just made the face and people understood, no words necessary.

Boone understood right away. His stuffed shirt chest rose and fell with the laughter of the old boys network. "Yeah. Know what you mean. My great-aunt Agnes had a better blond dye job than that one, but gotta say, the woman has one fine rack."

Andrew hmmmpped in a manner that would have made Old Lady Feldman proud, and Boone backpedaled appropriately.

Boone took a sip of his Scotch and sighed with regret. "But we can't go around evicting the tenants without cause. The rent laws are hell, not that I don't believe in bending the rules every now and then, especially for a friend like you, you know, but if she sued, we'd be slapped with some nuisance lawsuit, and you, my friend, well, those deep pockets of yours might be a few zeros lighter."

Andrew stroked his chin, pretending to mull things over. "She has some bad connections."

"Drugs, mob?" asked Boone.

"Both," said Andrew, deciding to fire both barrels at once.

"Hmm. That changes things. Gives us some cause in case she sues."

"I'd be willing to pay all her relocation expenses and some extra for her trouble. You know, just to keep the lawyers at bay."

"Yeah. God deliver us all from lawyers," laughed

Boone, who was a lawyer by trade, and a shark by genetic code.

"You'll see what you can do?" asked Andrew.

Boone clinked his glass against Andrew's. "Consider it done."

10

JEFF CALLED ANDREW for lunch on Thursday. Now, normally that was an easy answer.

No.

Jeff's idea of lunch usually involved the Sports-Zone or Hooters or both. Something with alcohol and flirty, blond waitresses who could be propositioned on the fly. So when Jeff suggested Cite Grill, Andrew knew something was seriously wrong.

It didn't take long to figure it out.

"She's driving me nuts!"

"Who?" asked Andrew mildly, thinking that whoever it was, he should pay them. Jeff didn't get distressed. Jeff had never had an ulcer. Jeff's idea of a tough life was choosing between a blonde or redhead. No, a little suffering would go a long way for Jeff.

"Sheldon Summerville."

Andrew gave him a chuck on the shoulder. "The party chick?"

Jeff shot him a look. "She thinks it's fun to trash the publisher of *Vanity Fair,* especially if it gets her in the papers."

Andrew put his chin on his palm, fascinated. "Really?"

"And that's not the worst of it. The party at South Beach. Skinny-dipping with the entire cast of *Ladies of Leisure*."

Andrew raised a brow. "I'm surprised that you objected."

"When her father first hired us, I thought, 'Okay, how hard could this be?' He wanted her to have this wholesome image—or at least a more wholesome image. Normally, hey, it's a free country, and if she chooses to flaunt her body in public, who am I to complain, but now—if he thinks I'm not doing my job, we lose the entire account. Do you how many zeroes are in this one, Andrew?"

"Seven?"

"Try ten, bro. Ten." Jeff pushed a hand through his dark hair as the waiter approached and took their order. "I'll have coffee. Black."

Coffee? This *was* serious. Jeff usually had a martini at lunch. Andrew looked up at the waiter. "Martini. Dry."

And Jeff didn't even notice. After the waiter left, Jeff continued the pity fest. "This party tomorrow. If she does something stupid, I'll kill her. I swear, I'll kill her myself."

"Have you tried to talk to her?"

"Oh, no, she's too busy for that. She has to shop. Shop! Stupid, brainless cow." Jeff waved a hand and Andrew tried not to laugh.

"Have you told any of this stuff to Mercedes?"

The look of horror on Jeff's face was nearly priceless, giving Andrew endless moments of blissful satisfaction. "Are you kidding? I'm trying to keep her name out of the papers. I've already bribed three gossip columnists to hush up the South Beach story. What would you do, Andrew?"

Now was a moment for the history books. Andrew steepled his fingers, assuming the wise, older brother "To keep her in line, you mean? You want my advice?"

"I know. I'm scraping bottom here. You have to help."

"Will she listen to her family?" asked Andrew, because he had heard in some American family circles, communication actually worked.

"Already tried."

"Business manager?"

"She fired him last week."

"You're screwed, my man."

"Andrew, you're the smartest person I know. Come on, you have to have some idea."

"Well…" said Andrew, tapping his fingers on the table. "There might be one way." Then he shook his head. "No. Never mind."

"Go on, tell me. I'll listen to anything. With the party tomorrow, some of the Yankees are going to be there. She loves the Yankees," he said mournfully.

"Oh," he said, as if that was the kiss of death. Sometimes life really was sweet. The waiter delivered their food and Andrew took special interest in his soup.

"So what's your idea?" asked Jeff, after Andrew had taken a mere two spoonfuls. It was a new record.

Andrew frowned thoughtfully. "No, you'd hate it."

"Tell me."

"I don't know."

"Can you just spit it out?"

Andrew put down his spoon. "All right. I think you should date her."

He might as well have said marry her. Jeff's mouth fell open. "You're insane."

"It just seemed expeditious. You could pretend to have a thing for her, draw her in on a tightrope, and hopefully she'd succumb to the infamous Brooks' charm. Of course, if you don't think you can do it…"

"That's a big pile of bull."

"So why not?"

"I don't even like her. She's not my style."

"Oh," said Andrew, who wondered when Jeff grew out of babes with big, bold headlights that just begged to be touched.

Instantly his brain zoomed to thoughts of Jamie, her hair down around her shoulders, big, bold…

Jeff snapped his fingers. "Hey. What do you think?"

Andrew pulled his thoughts to the present. "I'm sorry. You were talking to me?"

"Uh, no, I was talking to George Steinbrenner here in the seat next to me. Of course I was talking to you. I was explaining why your idea sucked."

"Because you don't think she'll say yes?"

Jeff looked indignant. "Of course she'll say yes."

"Just pretend, Jeff."

"We have an eight-month contract with her father.

I can't pretend for eight months. And then, after I break her heart, and she's determined to seek revenge, well, it's only going to get worse."

"You're right. She'd never want to go out with you."

"Yes, she would."

Andrew stayed silent, eating his soup.

"You don't think she would, do you?"

"You've got a pretty high opinion of yourself."

"Rightly deserved, thank you very much."

"If you say so."

"Fifty bucks, Andrew."

"For what?"

"Fifty bucks that she'll go out with me. Tomorrow. I'll tell her that I want it to be a real date."

Andrew kept his face down, eventually wiping all traces of a smile from his mouth. Finally he looked up. "You're on," he said, because yes, there was a God, and right now he was laughing his ass off.

THAT AFTERNOON, ANDREW LOOKED out his window and noticed a plane pulling a banner. Banners were a normal occurrence over New York harbor, but this one caught his eye.

HONEY-MOON, HONEY-MOAN, HONEY-MOAN FOR ME

Andrew blinked, cleared his vision, and hoped that perhaps his eyesight was giving out early. But when he opened his eyes, the banner was still there. He would have never suspected the fame and notoriety that a sex blog could bring to a woman. Thank God that his sister had stuck to fictional aliases. The better to hide behind, my dear.

Then one of his partners, Neil Harris, busted into his office. "Have you seen it today?" he asked, which was a normal question for Neil. He demanded his time at the watercooler and lived to be first to break the story. Usually the story was not-safe-for-work, which made Neil a very popular guy.

"What?" asked Andrew, because ignorance could sometimes be bliss.

"The Diaries. Dude, it sounds just like you!"

Andrew collapsed in the chair. "What do you mean?"

"Well, you're reading the diaries, right?"

"Yeah, sure," said Andrew, burying his head in his computer screen, pretending disinterest.

"But you haven't read today's, have you?"

A deep hellhole opened in front of him. Black, and bottomless, as deep and dark as his sister's heart. Andrew knew he wasn't sure he wanted to explore further, and if he'd been the only party involved, he would have done what he'd always done and ignored it. However, he had Honey's interest to think of, too.

"No," he muttered and returned back to his computer, because usually everyone left him alone when he buried himself in work.

Living in ignorance was a hard habit to break.

Neil settled in, hands flying. "Okay, so they're at the bar down on Front Street. Been there, there's like no action, if you know what I mean." Andrew scowled and Neil continued. "But back to Jack, they're eyeing each other, and he doesn't think anybody is watching, so he starts playing with her under the table."

Andrew coughed. "Can we skip the good parts? Can you tell me why it sounds like me?"

"Dark hair. Yale ring. Hedge fund. Whiz kid. And the dimple. It's you, man. You're Jack!"

It was a revealing he could have done without. But Andrew could always pull victory from the jaws of defeat. It was why he worked with hedge funds. He stared at Neil dispassionately and then burst out laughing. "That's a good one. You had me going for a minute."

Neil frowned. "I wasn't joking. It's you."

Andrew quirked a brow, condescending and arrogant. It was a look that he had mastered when speaking to investors, and they ate it up. Worked this time, too. Neil didn't look nearly so confident. "Do you know how many dark-haired, Yalies work at hedge funds?"

Neil's hands fell neatly in his lap. "Yeah. It was pretty far-fetched, wasn't it?"

Andrew laughed, but didn't think it was that far-fetched. If the world chose to believe he was a sexual dynamo, okay, it wasn't that out of the realm of possibility. In fact...

However, even his ego, touched as it was, didn't diminish the very real anger that was fast building inside him.

"Sorry, but I need to make a call. There's some numbers from the second quarter that Lyle is supposed to bring up for me." He checked his watch.

"The guy's fifteen minutes late. I think I'm going to dock his pay for that."

Neil rose and backed toward the door, laughing. "God, you're so right. Don't know what I was thinking."

Andrew forced a laugh and as soon as the office door closed, he picked up his phone and dialed.

TWO HOURS LATER they met on the roof of her building. After one look at the dread on Jamie's face, Andrew wanted to hit something. A wall, a computer screen, maybe his sister. He wasn't even a violent man. But Mercedes had gone too far. "I can't believe she did this."

Jamie winced. "It's all right. Does anybody know it's you?"

That was the worst of it. "In the last hour I've gotten thirty indecent e-mails and someone sent me edible underwear. Why not Jeff? I'm not the fun brother. I'm the stodgy brother. All my life I've done nothing but take care of her. Took care of them all, and this is what I get in return?"

"I'm sorry."

Instantly he stopped his tirade. "No, I'm sorry. You're safe, you know. My sister's a jerk, but she only hurts blood relatives. If it wasn't for the book deal…"

"She's writing a book?"

Andrew took her hand, wanting to calm her down, needing to touch her. "No, no, no. Not about us. I swear. I had called a friend at William-Morris, trying to do her a favor. I just wanted to help and this is what happens."

She raised her brows. "You have friends at William-Morris?"

They'd been after him to write an investing book, but who had the time? Andrew shrugged. "Casual acquaintances from school."

"Yale," she said quietly, her face not wearing the normal look of confidence. All because of Mercedes. "Did you tell her you were trying to help?"

Tell her? Mercedes? Andrew frowned. "She doesn't like me to interfere."

"Maybe she would this time. You should say something."

"Would you?"

"No."

And there you have it. "Didn't think so. I know when to keep my mouth shut. Look, I'm sorry that you got dragged into this. I'm a private person, Jamie. Very private. What's between you and me, I don't want anybody touching that. I don't want anybody talking about it. I don't want us to be watercooler fodder. You're too important to me for that." He needed her to believe this. "I had a great time this weekend, and I want more weekends. Lots more weekends."

There. He said it. Got it out in the open. He scanned her face, searching for some sign that she felt the same.

"You understand I have flaws?" she said, not the statement of undying love that he was looking for, but he understood. She was cautious. He was cautious.

"I like your flaws. I think your flaws are very sexy."

"Really?" she said, heat turning her eyes to pale blue fire. He could get lost in those fires. "I'm getting racier. Loosening up. Walking on the wild side."

He looked at her, noticing the flush on her cheeks. "Honey, I like your wild side just like it is." He gestured toward the plane. "Apparently somebody else does, too. Hiding secrets from me?"

She shrugged mysteriously and Andrew found himself charmed. "You didn't know about me and Lou Dobbs?"

Andrew rubbed his thumb against her palm. "I love it when you talk dirty to me."

She took a step closer. "T-Bills rose a quarter point today."

"Inflation?"

She reached down and cupped him. "Feels like it to me."

Andrew looked up overhead at the plane and coughed. "You're going to pay later."

She pretended to shiver. "Oh, scary man."

Andrew ran a wayward finger between the buttons of her blouse and then shook his head. Public displays of affection were what got them in trouble in the first place. "Are you okay?"

She pointed to the sky. "Because of that?"

Andrew nodded.

"Of course I'm fine. It's kind of fun having my name flown overhead in an airplane."

"Really?" he said, filing the detail away in his Jamie file in his head.

She scrunched her brows together. "Uh, no, thank you. That was a joke."

"Yeah, right. I knew that," he answered, striking the detail from the file. No planes. Limos only. "Speaking of weekend, we're still on, right?"

"Tomorrow night?"

"I'm thinking a long weekend."

She flicked her hair back, the confidence returning. "That could be arranged."

"We got invited to one of my brother's media events. *M* magazine. It's a big hoo-haw thing. Lots of media, lots of celebrity, lots of bling. That's not your style, is it? But you know, people get crazy about the idea of celeb stuff."

"Not me," she said.

"Afraid to be seen in public with Bull Market Jack?"

"The Hummer Honey is afraid of nothing."

"So that's a no, right?"

"That is correct."

Andrew blew out a breath. "Good, I hate that crap."

Her cell rang and she looked up apologetically. "It's my boss."

"Yeah, I got a meeting after the closing bell. I should be going," he said. But he didn't move and she didn't pick up the phone.

"Glad you came by," she said, and he took a step closer.

He took her in his arms, gave her a kiss. It started as a goodbye kiss, but she put a little extra hip action into it and turned it into a full-blown seduction. She came away flushed and out of breath. He came up away with a hard-on that was going to last for weeks.

"You're very dangerous, did you know that?"

She gave him a flirty wink. "You have no idea."

THURSDAY NIGHT WAS a busy night at 43C. Unfortunately, now that Andrew had convinced himself that Stella ran a co-op of ill repute, he was primed for every knock on the door, every quiet murmur in the hall that he knew represented a transaction of a sexual nature. Since he was going to have to wait another twenty-four hours, well, eighteen hours, before he negotiated any transactions of a sexual nature with Jamie, Stella's ongoing pleasure fest was really starting to piss him off.

When the next man hit the door knocker, Andrew jumped up from his desk and threw open the door. There, at the entrance to 43C stood a sixteen-year-old kid. The kid was pudgy, with dark hair that stood up in eighty different directions. In short, a kid that was never going to get laid. And here he was, standing at Stella's door, waiting to get his rocks off.

Now Andrew usually worked behind the scenes. It was his style, and he hated confrontations, but this was too much.

On the kid's back was a backpack, probably full of schoolbooks and his Batman lunchbox. "What're you doing here?" he asked, hoping to shame the kid into leaving.

The kid flushed bright red, and Andrew shook his

head. "Why don't you leave while you still can? You're too young for this."

That brought the kid's head up. "I'm not too young. You adults think you know everything. Give me a break. Just stay out of my business, mister."

Right then, Stella opened her door. "Excuse me? Brad? Is there a problem?"

The kid shot Andrew a go-to-hell look. "Not at all."

Andrew took in the usual pink robe, the fresh-faced kid who was probably still a virgin, and knew he couldn't let it go. Not this time. This was wrong, and Jamie would want him to interfere.

"What are you doing with a kid that age? I've watched while you go about your business with all the other men, but you can't mess with kids." He stabbed a finger in the air. "There're laws against that."

"What in God's name are you talking about?" asked Stella, suddenly finding religion. How convenient.

"Do you think we don't know what's going on inside that apartment? Everybody knows."

The kid's eyes grew wide. "You know?" He turned to Stella. "You said you would keep the whole thing confidential."

"I didn't tell him," she said and then walked out into the hallway, a crocheted scarf trailing behind her. God only knows what she did with the scarf. "Exactly what are you implying, Mr. Brooks?"

"You. The kid. I saw *The Graduate*. I don't think I need to say any more."

She stared, her face growing white. "You should be ashamed of yourself."

Down the hallway, Old Lady Feldman peered beyond her security chain. Andrew gave her a reassuring glance. He had everything under control. "I'm not the one...well, you know what you're doing."

"She's giving me knitting lessons," yelled the kid, and suddenly doors opened up all up and down the hallway.

"Knitting lessons?" scoffed Andrew. "That's a new one."

Then the kid pulled open his backpack and brought out a roll of yarn and yes, knitting needles.

Stella stared at Andrew, as if he'd just condemned her to well, what he just condemned her to. "Knitting lessons? Only for men?" he asked, raising an eyebrow.

"I run a business called Men in Stitches. I focus on teaching knitting, crochet, sewing and trim accessories to men who are too embarrassed to take a class from a regular sewing school."

"Trim accessories?" repeated Andrew.

She nodded. "I like rhinestones, but very few men really go for that much bling. Mainly patches, leather, customized embroidery. That sort of thing."

Andrew looked up and noticed that the doors on the hallway were all now closed. Leaving him alone, feeling about the size of a pissant. "I owe you an apology," he said. Then he remembered Boone and the impending eviction. "And there's another little problem you might run into."

Stella stamped a little rhinestone-encrusted shoe. It

was nicely done, he noticed. "Haven't you done enough?"

He blew out a breath. "Not yet. But trust me. I'll get it all taken care of."

FRIDAY STARTED BADLY. There was a voice mail from Sandy the not-so-much-a-Gorgon-anymore.

"Sorry to do this to you, Jamie, but Arnie got called out on a meeting. It's not really a meeting, but actually a pro basketball cheerleader that he targeted for his latest sexual merger and acquisition, but you didn't hear it from me."

Immediately Jamie called her back.

"Sandy, I need this meeting. Tell me he's there."

"He's here, but he's waiting on a call from some magazine editor. Said cheerleader is going to be at some event this evening and he wants to go."

"You've got to be kidding me. He's ditching me because he's trying to get into the skirt of some cheerleader?"

"Men are dogs."

Not all of them. Then her brain backed up. "Wait a minute. What party?"

"*M* magazine."

Oh. My. God. Jamie blew out a breath. "Sandy, what if I get him an invite?"

"You'll be his hero."

"I can get him an invite," she said, definitively, matter-of-factly, as if she delved in high society malfunctions everyday. Jamie McNamara was back, in charge, soaring through business like an eagle on steroids.

"Oh, girl, he's going to love you. But watch his hands. I'm too old for him to hit on, but don't think I don't see it."

Oh, yeah, she knew the type. She'd heard the rumors. Techazoid geek billionaire trying to run with the bulls and not quite making it. In New York, money makes up for many deficiencies, but not all of them.

"Don't worry about me. I'm involved," said Jamie, savoring the words. Involved. Yes, she was involved, with Andrew. Master of the deal. Master of her heart. Sappy, but true. So he was better at investments than she was? So what? So he was on the cover of *Forbes* as an annual occurrence? So what? No biggie. Not a problem. She was an adult, she could deal.

After getting the green light from Newhouse, she called Andrew. Just at the sound of his voice something inside her turned to goo. She explained the situation, and Andrew didn't even quibble. Of course they would go. He knew how important this deal was to her, which was the marvelous thing about Andrew.

He knew how important this deal was to her.

Her toes curled inside her classical, black slingbacks, the deep voice tossing around terms like rate of return and zero-coupon bonds, and in general, getting her all wet.

She really couldn't wait for tonight, and it had nothing to do with Newhouse, and everything to do with Andrew. He stayed on the line, seducing her with his analysis of pork belly futures. Eventually he had to hang up because he had a call with the UK that he couldn't get out of. Jamie invented an overseas call of her own.

For a few minutes she stared silently at the phone, her toes slowing uncurling.

He wasn't jealous of the time she spent jetting around the U.S., mainly because he jetted more. He wasn't jealous of her client base, mainly because he had more. He wasn't jealous of her magazine covers, mainly because, oh, right, she didn't make the covers of business mags.

Oh, piddle.

Jamie dashed her doubts into the trash and did something she'd been waiting to do for twelve solid months. She strode into Walter's office, giving Helen a "this is important" nod. This was Jamie McNamara, heels down, figures flying, data-spouting Jamie McNamara, who always got her man.

"Walter, great news," she said, palms down on his desk. "I'm seeing Newhouse tonight. Wrangled him an invitation that he's been wanting."

Walter stood and clapped her on the back. "That's the Jamie McNamara that I know and love. He'll never survive your fastball, Jamie."

"No, sir," she answered and threw him an imaginary pitch. He pulled out his bottle of Scotch to celebrate and this time Jamie participated. She was in.

Yup, everything was fine and dandy. No reason to worry. No reason at all.

11

THAT NIGHT, ANDREW ARRIVED at Jamie's apartment, prepared for many things, but seeing Jamie dressed in black, with cleavage, substantial, bountiful cleavage, pulled him back in time, to his earlier years, before he learned how to form words.

"Oh," he said.

She frowned. "You don't like?"

He blinked, clearing the burn from his retinas. "Like is such a mild-mannered word. Like is for mint chocolate chip ice cream, flannel sheets and Mel Brooks movies. Let's find something more fitting," he said, watching the way the dress fitted each and every curve. "Heart-pounding, blood-pumping, eyeball-goggling, Johnson-lifting, oh-God-kill-me-now-while-I'm-a-happy-man."

She started to giggle. "That's more than one word."

"I was never good at English," he said, coming forward and taking her in his arms. "Math. That's where my interests belonged. Numbers. Figures. Curves. Breasts."

He nibbled at her neck, his hand sliding forward

to just slip under the neckline and possibly cop a feel.

"Oh, Honey," he said, deciding that life really didn't get better than this.

"Oh, Jack," she answered, copping a feel of her own.

"How much time do we have?" he said, sliding one strap down her arm, giving him a peek at one pink nipple that just begged for attention.

"None," she said, but he couldn't help himself, he bent his head to take the ripe flesh in his mouth. Her head fell back, offering him up even more, and he didn't hesitate at all. Slowly he sucked at the nipple, her low moans the most seductive of all turn-ons. Why did they want to go to a party? Damn, the real party was right here, with Jamie in his arms. He slid one hand down her waist, but she stopped him before he could explore farther.

Furthering his disappointment, she slid the strap back over her shoulder. "Not enough time. Later. I swear. Extravagant sexual favors will be exchanged."

"How extravagant?"

She gave him a sultry smile. "Heavy crude."

Andrew slapped a hand over his heart. "You do that on purpose, don't you?"

She didn't answer, merely flipped up the back of her skirt, exposing nothing but one most fabulous derriere, framed by a pair of black, silk stockings and four-inch black heels.

All intelligible thoughts fled his brain, replaced by one primitive desire to plant himself right at the apex of her thighs.

He reached for her, but she was too quick, dancing just out of his reach. But Andrew was a patient man. He knew the value of timing. He would wait.

He locked her door and watched her walk, hips swaying in a rhythm that hypnotized him.

He closed his eyes, ordered his cock to stand down, and then went on his way.

Did he mention the waiting was hell?

THEY TOOK A CAB to the party at the hotel. Andrew considered a Hummer limo, but because of the rumors, wisely decided against it. Jamie would never know how close she came to getting some big-cap action in a Hummer limo—twice.

The hotel was one of those sleek, modernistic things that cost an arm and a leg, and you could usually find a statue of an arm and leg posing as the artwork in the lobby. Green lighting surrounded the front entrance, and there was lots of chrome and glass. All in all, it reminded Andrew of a big flower vase.

When they entered the lobby, the flashbulbs began to click. Going off in his eyes, blinding him. Unfortunately, his hearing hadn't diminished at all.

"Bull Market Jack!"

"Is she the Hummer Honey?"

"Mr. Brooks, are you really Bull Market Jack?"

"Mr. Brooks, E! Entertainment Network!"

"Mr. Brooks, CNBC! We've heard rumors of insider trading? Care to comment?"

He heard Jamie's indrawn breath and realized that

he'd never considered the barracuda quality of the tabloids. Damn.

"I'm sorry," he whispered in her ear. "Trust me. I can fix this."

She shot him a look, doubtful, yet trusting. Good instincts on Wall Street. In that one moment, he saw her head warring with her heart, and he understood. And he'd never loved her more because of that.

Blind trust. In the world of financial trading, when you live and die by the bottom line, where facts stand alone, there are no such thing as doubts, only risk. Trust was like water in the desert. A mirage that didn't exist.

Andrew had never asked that anyone trust him. When he was growing up, trust really didn't matter. No one trusted that Andrew would pay the rent, he just did. Andrew Brooks. Reliable. Dependable. Steadfast.

He took his reading glasses from his pocket and put them halfway down his nose. Then he held up a quieting hand and there were lots of shushing noises.

"Ladies and gentleman of the press, I've heard the rumors, read the stories, but let me be the first to say: I drive a Toyota with the highest insurance deductible allowed by law. I'm a firm believer in certificates of deposit, and I think that the Hummer as a consumer vehicle is an ecological equivalent of the Queen Mary. You really think I'm this super stud-launcher? Well, I'm flattered, but my burning question for you all is, what the hell have you been smoking?"

There was a heart-stopping silence as he waited to

see if anyone believed him. Then from the back of the room, embarrassed tittering broke out, and the doubts began to surface. Andrew began to breathe again and then finally, sensing the story opportunity had burst, the crowd began to dwindle away. Quickly he stored his glasses back in his jacket. God he hated the things.

Jamie looked at him, eyeing him up and down. "Well, hell. I was considering buying a Hummer with my year-end bonus."

He squeezed her hand. "You want a Hummer, Honey? Just wait till later."

Just then, a man approached, right hand outstretched to Andrew. Good-looking in a well-tailored, Princeton sort of way. Golden blond hair that women really seemed to go for and a cleft chin. Gads. Andrew shook his hand and sighed.

"Andrew Brooks."

"Arnold Newhouse. Damn glad to meet you. I've read about your research strategies. Fascinating. Using an inverted price per earnings ratio instead of more traditional metrics."

"You're here to meet with Jamie," reminded Andrew, noticing the way her brows were furrowed together.

Jamie held out a hand. "You have a few moments to talk?"

Arnie looked like he would say no, but Andrew intervened. "You both sit down. I'll get drinks," he said, taking off before Arnie could follow him.

He watched from the second level, seeing Jamie in action. God, she was prime. Even Arnie looked impressed, but after ten minutes, Andrew knew she was losing him. However, the night was young.

Back downstairs, he noticed the tiny lines on Jamie's forehead and he longed to smooth them all away. This really wasn't fair. Not after all her hard work. Andrew squeezed her hand, wanting to tell her that everything would be fine. She smiled, but this time the smile didn't meet her eyes.

They took the escalator to the mezzanine level and Arnie pulled even with him. "Listen, I want to set up a lunch. You, me, maybe one of your analysts. I've been meaning to give you a call, and tonight is just serendipity."

Andrew looked down at Jamie who was riding on the step behind them, looking even more forbidding. Then he looked back at Arnie. "We're pretty well booked. Bond-Worthington, now that's the firm you need to look at."

Jamie broke into a fit of coughing.

Why did things always have to be complicated? He sensed that Jamie and complications were one and the same and he was just going to have to get used to it.

He took her hand, cast an apologetic look at Arnie, and moved her behind some large-ass plant thing.

"Don't worry," he said, guessing that with a few well-placed compliments about Jamie's encyclopedic knowledge base, Arnie would be eating out of her hands. "I can fix this."

"How?" she asked, her face filled not with gratitude but suspicion.

"I'll tell him how great you are, what a fine job Bond-Worthington does, how the firm is the leader in capital management. He'll listen to me."

And rather than complimenting him on the brilliant genius of his plan, her eyes began to fill with tears. "I can't do this, Andrew."

"What 'this' are we talking about? The party?" he asked hopefully.

"Andrew, it's going to be like this everywhere, isn't it?"

"It's not too bad. You get used to it after a while," he said, because although he did get some attention within the financial circles, mainly it was more annoying than anything.

She looked up at him and wiped at her cheeks. "I've always been proud of what I've done, I've always known my goals and my capabilities, and I've always delivered. Always. And now I'm doubting myself. It seems like everyone is better than me. You, Stephanie, hell, even Lindsey's going great guns at work."

"Jamie, you can't do this to yourself. Doubts are just wasted energy. Let me talk to him."

"That's the problem, Andrew. I don't want you to have to fix things for me. I should be fixing problems."

"And you can, of course you can," he said, pulling her into his arms, holding her tight. This was a side of her he hadn't seen before. She'd always been so self-confident and self-assured, and now, like this, he wanted to protect her, to shelter her, to make every-thing better. And before the night was over, he would.

Before the night was out, Arnie Newhouse would be a client of Bond-Worthington, if Andrew had anything to do with it.

He pressed a kiss in her hair, loving the way she fit him so perfectly. She was tough, strong, sexy, but underneath was nothing but marshmallow. She turned him upside down and inside out, but Jamie McNamara was his. Forever.

"Jamie, everything will be all right. I swear. Tonight, let's just have a good time, right?"

She sniffed and then nodded. "I can't believe I'm crying like this. A McNamara doesn't cry. Ever."

He gave her a kiss, trying to get a smile back on her face. "I'll never tell. Swear."

THE ENTIRE MEZZANINE LEVEL was completely decorated in silver ribbon wherever you looked, silver apparently being the signature color for *M* Magazine. The alcohol was flowing freely, served by faux blondes, with silver-painted skin, and possibly nothing underneath. The whole thing was massively overdone. There was something to be said for leaving a little to the imagination and whenever Andrew's eyes lingered on the trim, yet tight lines of her dress, Jamie knew she had found the right mix.

Andrew went off looking for his brother, giving her some more quality time with Newhouse.

"So," she asked Arnie, "what do you think of the spread?"

He leaned back on Italian wing-tipped heels. "Fab,

absolutely, fab," he murmured, scarfing a passing martini from a waitress and then downing it.

"I think it's important for a financial company to be dynamic and modern, able to adapt to the changing times," Jamie answered, watching in fascination as a waitress climbed up on the dance floor, and began performing sexual acts against a pole. Jamie had read about New York nightlife, but experiencing it, firsthand, didn't prepare her for how people could be so...public.

Arnie nodded his head, and Jamie assumed it was in agreement, until she realized he was shifting in rhythm with the waitress on the pole. Sadly, escapades such as this signaled the downfall of any ethical standards the business community ever possessed. It was very difficult to talk business with a man who was thinking with his small head, rather than his large one, and the pain began to pound in her head, and she pulled a martini off a passing tray.

"I understand that you're interested in basketball," said Jamie, deciding that casual conversation might be the best tactic.

"Are you a fan?" he asked, his eyes scanning the crowd.

Jamie sighed, deciding that a wise woman knows when she's beaten. "She's over there," she said, pointing to the tiny platinum blonde with the cheerleader smile.

He took off in the direction of his heart's desire, and Jamie snagged a waitress. "Excuse me, do you have anything with chocolate?"

12

ANDREW FOUND HIS SISTER near the main bar. "I thought you couldn't come?"

Mercedes flushed. "I thought I had a date, but then he ditched me. Decided this would be better than sitting home alone."

"Anything else?" he said, not even close to forgiving her.

"Sorry."

"For what?" he said, because he wanted to extract as much pain as humanly possible.

"You didn't deserve it," she muttered.

"So why'd you do it then?"

"You ticked me off."

"Oh, yeah, that's right. I tick you off, so you must blast my sexual exploits with a megaphone."

"Made-up sexual exploits," she corrected.

"Not all of them," he reminded her.

She raised a brow. "Should we start calling you Jack?"

He glared.

Just then a waitress appeared. "Drinks, ma'am?" she said, and then cast a sultry look in Andrew's direction. "Anything for you? Jack?" she said, her hand depositing something in his pocket.

Mercedes snorted. "This isn't Jack. Trust me," she said, then lowered her voice. "Trust me."

The waitress ran off, leaving them alone. Andrew cast a sideways look at Mercedes. "You really didn't need to emasculate me there. Simple denial would have been good." Then he fished in the contents of his pocket, pulling out a small garage door opener looking device. "What is this? A hotel key?"

His sister started to laugh. "It's a remote control. For a vibrator."

He looked at it carefully. "You're kidding? They have those?"

She rolled her eyes. "You are such a babe in the woods. It's a good thing I'm not going to use Jack and Honey anymore, because you are absolutely no help."

Andrew stared, intrigued by this half-assed olive branch. "You're pulling the Web site?"

"Not the Web site. Just Jack and Honey. You're in luck. William-Morris wants a deal, and he said I needed to find another hook. That Honey and Jack would be passé by the time we shopped a manuscript."

"Smart man, you should listen to him."

"I've already taken the stories down," she said.

"Good," he said, supremely satisfied that once again life was back in its natural balance. "Sorry about the date. He must be a jerk."

"They're all jerks. Present company excluded—at least most of the time," she said.

Andrew nodded. "Thank you for that vote of confidence. Where did you get that?" he asked, noticing the press pass around her neck.

"From him," she said, pointing her thumb at Jeff, who was sitting anxiously in a corner.

Andrew looked harder, because Jeff's face never lost that self-assured confidence—until now. "What's he doing there?"

Mercedes gave him a wide smile. "See the woman at the bar?"

And there Andrew saw the reason for Jeff's anxiety attack. For a moment, he felt something that in a less hard-hearted man would be termed sympathy. The woman had climbed up on the bar and was "dancing." Dancing being a rhetorical term only because actually it was more of a visual seduction. She was grinding, rubbing, pulsing, throbbing, and every other "ing" ever invented to cover the primal mating ritual. And the men were lapping it up, tongues hanging out, each and every one drawn into her web. And there was Jeff. Her date.

Andrew rubbed his hands together, and Mercedes looked at him, suspicion in her eyes. "Why do you look so happy?"

"This was my idea," he said proudly.

"Get her drunk and let her have her way with every male in the joint?"

"No, I told him he should date her. That's Sheldon Summerville?"

"In the uh-hum, flesh."

"Wow," was all Andrew could say. She wore a skintight dress that showed in a very precise manner exactly how the cold was affecting her. The skirt billowed out around her as she danced, exposing legs the length of California, most of Oregon being exposed as well.

"I'm not sure she thinks Jeff is her date," said Mercedes, watching as Sheldon jumped down from the bar, sliding into the arms of some big, bulging bozo, whom she kissed on the ear and then swatted away.

"Just wait," said Andrew, with all the authority of someone who had already seen the end of this movie.

Sheldon landed into Jeff's lap, straddling him. Jeff tried to move her legs to one side, but Sheldon was a woman who knew her mind, and she refused to budge.

"Who do you think's going to win?" he asked.

"My money's on Sheldon. I don't think I've ever seen a woman quite so limber," she said, tilting her head as the bombshell leaned backward.

Andrew pulled out a ten. "I have to bet on blood."

"You're only putting down ten?"

"Gambling is a crappy investment. Give me fifty, and I'll get you twenty percent in eighteen months."

"Sometimes I don't believe we're related. I can't even make my rent."

Andrew turned around, surprised. "I thought you had two roommates."

Mercedes looked away. "I kicked them out."

"Mercedes, you can't afford the rent on your own."

"They were shooting up. What do you propose I do, hmm?"

And he had the grace to feel ashamed. "Well, okay. I guess that's the correct course of action. Have you put up notices?"

"I'm going to try and live alone for a while. I mean, it works for you, Jeff and Mom."

"Jeff and I have jobs."

"Save the lectures, Andrew. All right. I have a job, too."

"Really?"

"Yeah," she said and then her smile curved slyly. "Writing a column for the *Herald*."

Andrew gave her a hug. "I knew you could do it," he said, because he knew the editor for the *Herald*, too. God knows, his sister should be doing something more honorable than writing sex books.

She beat him on the back. "Oh, puh-lease. You told me I needed to find a real profession."

"Well, yes, but that was before you got a real job."

"Look!" Mercedes turned back to the bar. "Andrew, I think you're going to lose. That wasn't a kiss, that was a tonsillectomy."

Andrew squinted. "Aren't there laws against that?"

"Only in Utah. And speaking of…when do I meet the date?"

"Jamie?"

"The Hummer Babe."

"Please call her Jamie. She's very nice, and she blushes easily."

"Really?"

"No, but I expect you to be nice to her. And be on your best behavior, because there's a client with her that she's trying to impress. Actually, he might be a good match for you."

Andrew had tried to divert her from the "client with her" part, but Mercedes, damn her hide, picked right up on it, in that annoying way that family members often do. "She brought someone else with her? Male or female?"

"Why does that matter?"

"Male, huh?"

Andrew nodded. "It's business."

"A regular corporate soldier, isn't she?"

Spoken like someone who'd never spent any time managing to survive in the real world. "She's ambitious."

Mercedes narrowed her eyes. "How ambitious?"

"Not that ambitious."

"Good, because if I thought she was using my big brother to advance her own career, well, I'd have to kick her ass."

Andrew laughed. "You couldn't kick Pooh's ass, Mercedes."

"I want to meet her, Andrew, and if I don't approve…" His little sister looked at him curiously.

"You'll what?"

"Why, I think I'll have to revoke your allowance."

IT TOOK ABOUT TEN minutes for Mercedes to figure out how to get Andrew to stop hovering over Jamie and leave them alone in order to further the inquisition. The Hummer Honey. And woo-wee, this woman did not look the type to do *anything* in a Hummer limo, much less ma-nana-nana. Finally, Mercedes told her brother that she needed a banana daiquiri with Captain Morgan rum, kosher salt and a pineapple, lime, kiwi, mango medley on the side. "And make sure the bartender gets it right, will you?"

He looked at her strangely. "You're not pregnant, are you?"

Mercedes gaped. "Not in this lifetime, bro. You want to be an uncle, get Jeff to spawn," she said, and watched him go off, leaving Mercedes alone with her prey.

"So, you're my brother's latest?" Mercedes had decided it was best to start out on the offensive, then work up from there.

"Latest?" asked Jamie nervously.

Good, good. It's better if the subject realizes right off the bat that they're being put under a nuclear-powered microscope. Mercedes pushed back the bangs from her eyes. "Oh, yeah. Don't let that stuffy, I-can't-get-a-date pretense fool you. He's a randy sort, and the women love the money. In fact, most of the women that he goes out with see themselves as the next Mrs. Andrew Brooks."

"The next? Was there a first Mrs. Andrew Brooks?"

"Oh, yeah," said Mercedes, really starting to get into it. "He drove her mad and then institutionalized her."

"Oh, yeah. I read that. *In Wuthering Heights.*"

Okay, one point for the away team. "You read the classics?"

"Mainly *Cliff Notes*. It's much more efficient," said Jamie, which sounded so much like Andrew that

Mercedes looked twice. Zounds, maybe there was something between these two.

"Very impressive."

"Not really. I took twenty-two hour semesters and I couldn't do all the reading and manage the six hours of sleep that I needed in order to function at peak capacity. Something had to be done, and once I realized that I could cut my reading time by seventy-three percent, well, it was a no-brainer. I did read Twain, though. For fun," she added.

"Hated Twain. Socialist, Marxist, pinko."

"Mark Twain?"

"Oh, yeah," said Mercedes. "You didn't know?"

"Are you lying to me?"

"Maybe."

"Do you do this to all the girls your brother dates?"

"Only the ones that make him loopy."

"I make him loopy?" she asked, a pleased smile on her face.

Whoa. Too much ammunition for the enemy. Rewind. "It's either that or all the mercury."

"What mercury?"

"Fish. Andrew was a huge fish eater as a child and every now and then, when the moon phases kick in just right, his mercury levels rise and he just goes right over the top."

"I don't believe you."

"It's your right," said Mercedes with a careless shrug, "but if you're going to fit in with the family, you have to—"

"Arnie!" cried Jamie, and then she ran off after some blond-haired dude who was posing for a photographer for the magazine and Mercedes was left alone until Andrew returned with the fruit salad drink.

"I think I got everything you asked for. Had to tip him a fifty," he groused. "What do you think of Jamie?" he asked, which meant things were serious. Much more serious than Mercedes had assumed.

She had thought Jamie would've been some bubble-headed party doll—like Jeff's date, but Jamie wasn't like that at all. Which worried Mercedes because Andrew needed someone lively, someone with personality, someone who would lift him out of his old-fogeyness. She studied him and sighed.

"What does that mean? You don't like her?"

"You don't care what I think," said Mercedes, gnawing on a piece of pineapple.

"That means you don't like her. You know, it's the client thing that's got her all wound up."

"She's not normally like this?"

Andrew thought for a moment. "No, she normally is. But I like her that way," he added.

"Andrew, have you ever thought about dating a woman who was opposite of you? Someone more— uh, how do I put it? Fun?"

"I have fun," he muttered.

"Your idea of fun is saving ten percent on your car insurance."

He glared. "And why do you have a problem with sound fiscal policy? Just because I don't burn through the cash like it's toilet paper doesn't mean I'm not a fun person."

She gave him an even look. "You are *so* not a fun person."

"If your idea of fun is making up stories about innocent people and selling personal information for thirteen pieces of silver to the first publisher that comes along and asks—"

"That is not true and you know it. I'm a writer, and I don't have a contract for my book—yet."

"So why don't you write a real book?" he said. "Instead of some cheesy sex book?"

She pointed a finger at his chest. "This is why you are not a fun person. There is nothing wrong with writing a cheesy, sex book, and it's not cheesy, thank you very much."

"I read what you wrote, Mercedes. It's pretty cheesy."

"You're such a man," she answered, because there was really no insult that could top that one.

"Are you going to eat that kiwi?" he asked and took it from her drink.

She glared at her brother and munched the lime unhappily. God, maybe he and Jamie deserved each other, after all.

ARNIE NEWHOUSE WAS everything that annoyed Andrew, wrapped up in one Ivy-Leaguered package. Smooth, confident, and reeking of money. Earlier, he had his arm wrapped around some young blonde, but then sent her away after Jamie left.

Andrew knew the drill and nodded. "Nice," he said. "I love a woman with big—"

Andrew interrupted. "She left something for you."

Arnie looked intrigued. "Really?"

Andrew passed over the vibrator remote in a suitably manly manner.

Arnie, damn him, immediately knew what it was. He stared at the piece of plastic, worship in his eyes. "She wants me."

Andrew nodded. "Definitely. Listen, do you mind if we talk business for a minute?"

Arnie pulled himself out of vibrator-nirvana, dollar signs in his eyes. "No, go ahead."

"I thought you might have some questions. I know that Jamie's been talking to you about B&W and their programs. Great firm."

Arnie didn't take the bait. "You just work with small-caps, don't you?"

And yes, we have another hedge fund groupie. Hallelujah and pass the peanut butter. Andrew took a long sip of Scotch. The better to endure. "I think the large-caps are overbought. To drive the returns like we do at SBPB, you have to find stocks that haven't been picked over. Small-caps give us that competitive advantage."

"What sort of growth rates are you looking for?"

"The big rockets. A jump between thirty and forty percent ideally."

"And you use the momentum to cash in, right?"

"Yeah."

"So, if I wanted to find out about some of the companies that were about to take off…."

"You'd hire someone."

"Like SBPB?"

Mweep. Wrong answer. "Like Bond-Worthington. Jamie is the best."

"You don't think I have the resources for SBPB, is that it?" asked Arnie, looking over the rim of his glass.

"I'm sure you do," laughed Andrew. "But SBPB isn't the workhorse capital management firm that B&W is. I've read about your style of investing, Newhouse. I think B&W is a good fit."

"You've read up on me?"

"Sure," lied Andrew. "There was that piece in…oh, you know…" He looked away.

"*Connecticut Today?*"

Andrew snapped his fingers. "That's the one!"

Arnie shrugged silk-covered shoulders. "They did okay, but I think I'd like to talk to you more about investing at SBPB."

And out of the corner of his eye, he noticed Jamie approaching. Time to close this deal and fast. Andrew had plans for the evening and Arnie Newhouse was not part of them. "Look, I'm about to give you the opportunity of a lifetime. Sign on with B&W. Tell Jamie tonight. In return, I'll send you a weekly e-mail for a year. Buy/sell recommendations and a complete breakdown of the market watch on each company. You have questions, you pick up the phone and call me. Gratis. No transaction fees, no management fees. Nada."

Arnie's blue eyes turned green. It didn't take a college man to realize what he was being offered. "And you're doing this, why?"

Jamie was getting closer, and Andrew felt pressure burning in his gut. "Take it or leave it and not a word to Jamie, other than the fact that you're signing."

Arnie watched as Jamie approached, and Andrew felt the sweat start to bead on the back of his neck. "She must be quite talented, your Jamie."

Andrew fisted his hands, but then Jamie came up to stand next to him. "Miss me?" she asked cheerfully, with a curious glance to Arnie.

"Of course," he said and slipped an arm around her, taking a moment to give Arnie a long look.

"Jamie, I think I have some news that you've been wanting to hear," said Arnie.

"And what is that?" asked Jamie coolly. Never a hair out of place. Andrew looked on with pride.

"I've decided to move our assets over to B&W. I'm assuming that you'd be agreeable."

Only Andrew felt the telltale jump in her body. But she looked at Newhouse and nodded. "Of course. But tonight isn't about business, is it? Let's just relax and enjoy the party. Business can wait."

And the entire time she was talking, her hand was slowly cutting off the circulation to his fingers. Damn, he loved this woman.

WHILE ARNIE WAS dancing with his cheerleader, Jamie took Andrew by the hand and led him over to a far corner on the upper level, letting out the scream that had built up inside her.

"Oh, my God! I did it. Did you see his face? I can't believe it. I wasn't sure that he'd bite after that pitch earlier, I thought, you know, throw a few numbers his way, whet the whistle, and then follow up with a lunch meeting in a week, and then do the day-long presentation in a month. I have a standard schedule that I use to close the deal. But this!" Jamie rubbed a hand over her face. "I've never closed anything this fast."

Andrew watched her indulgently. "You should wear that dress for all your client meetings."

Instantly the brows drew together. "You don't think it's a sex thing, do you?"

Andrew backtracked. "Nah. It's you. You inspire trust in investors, Jamie. Very simple. And it's very important in this day and age for people to feel that trust."

"Do you really think so?"

"Of course," said Andrew, backing her into the corner because it had been forty-five minutes since he kissed her and he wanted to see if she still tasted the same. He caught her lips and pulled her close, intending to start with something sweet, tender, romantic.

But Jamie had different ideas. One flirtatious leg caught in between his thighs and began to rub against places that women didn't need to tease. Instantly, his cock sprang to demanding life.

"How long do we have to stay here?"

"Until eleven at least," she whispered in his ear, using a persuasive length of tongue, too. The saucy minx.

"I can't walk back downstairs in this condition, Jamie," he said, hoping that she'd consider ducking out early.

"I have a better idea," she said, taking his hand and leading him back toward the stairs.

"Where are you taking me?" he asked, not really caring where they were going if the spark in her eyes was any indication.

THERE WAS SOMETHING utterly naughty about finally breeching the porcelain confines of the men's restroom. Other women might aspire to the boardroom, but Jamie had always suspected that most deals were sealed in the men's room. And tonight she wanted to seal one of her own, in a very, kinky (at least for Jamie) manner.

The place was remarkable, all sparkling chrome and ebony, and a long, long, long line of stalls.

Happily she led him into the stall at the end, and as soon as the door was closed and locked, they met in a furious melding of lips, skin and passion. She ran her hands under his shirt, sending one button flying under the wall.

"Forgive me," she said, her hands at his fly.

"You're kidding, right?" he asked, sliding down the straps to her dress, and palming her breasts in his hand. "Jamie, how is a man supposed to have a decent quarter, when all he can think about is this?"

His hands pulled at her nipples, and she leaned against the door, letting him have his way with her, his hands caressing her carefully.

He bent lower, his mouth closing over one full breast and he began to suck, each pull of his mouth shooting waves of pleasure directly between her legs. She rubbed against one strong thigh, trying to ease the itch that was building inside her.

She was vaguely aware of the door opening to the men's room, but all she could hear was the sound of her blood, pulsing and firing like a shot. His lips covered the other nipple, sucking even harder, and she muffled the pleasure-sound that was threatening to burst out from inside her.

Needing to find relief, she ran her hands inside his pants, finding the strong erection bursting from his briefs (white, of course). She pulled it free, running her hands up and down, milking him until he raised his head, his dark eyes deep and full of intent.

He raised her skirt and pulled one leg high around his waist, using his other hand to thrust himself inside her in one sharp move.

She froze.

He stopped. "Are you okay?" he whispered.

She nodded, because speech was currently impossible, and then he began to move, pushing thickly inside her, each thrust slow and deep. She held onto his shoulders, needing to find something immovable because it seemed as if the world was going to fly off the axis each time she felt him move.

The water ran in the sink as the unknown occupant came and went, and soon the door closed, and they were alone again.

"Do you think he noticed?" she asked.

"If he did, I'm sure he's jealous," he said, and she struggled to get her hips in closer.

"This isn't working," she told him.

"Not a problem," he told her, and then moved her in front of him, spreading her hands on the back wall. "I used to be a cop in another life."

Jamie giggled. "You're just like your sister."

"That's a fine way to ruin a man's sexual fantasies," he said, and then lifted her dress.

"Oh, Honey," he whispered, and then moved behind her, thrusting in slowly, inch by inch, piercing through her.

"Much better," she said, with approval, and his arms wrapped around her, his fingertips just barely grazing her nipples. She felt a shiver rip through her, and he thrust again, thick inside.

Their bodies moved together, entwined by a bond that she felt in her heart.

His lips found her neck and he nuzzled her skin, tickling her, making her feel adored. Did he know what he was doing to her insides?

His hand moved in front of her, down to where their bodies were joined, and when his finger began to stroke her clit, very efficient, very determined, searching her very soul, she knew that he was claiming much more than her body.

Slowly the fears began to subside and the sensual waves lapped over her, and she began to relax, to simply feel the pleasure of having a man inside her. Not any man. Andrew.

His strokes came faster and his thumb matched the rhythm of his cock. She felt her orgasm climbing higher and higher, and she fought it, because she wasn't a screamer and she wasn't about to be turned into one in a bathroom stall, but the darkness was approaching behind her eyes and her breathing turned heavy and staggered.

"Oh, Jamie. Honey," he said, his own voice deep and ragged.

Her hands clutched the tile in front of her, searching for balance and order, finding none. The darkness came and as he thrust inside her one last time, she felt her climax burst like a dam. Warm waters rushed through her, and he took her even further, another climax following on the heels of the first. She was going to scream. She knew she was going to scream, and this was really not the time for her to scream.

His arms tightened, his body jerked, and in Andrew's arms, she knew there was safety, security, and a place where she had never been.

He could make her forget her plans, her goals, her dreams. He made her forget everything but him.

"I love you, Jamie," he whispered. "I know it's fast, I know it's radical, but I've never been like this before."

Her fingers slid down the cold tile and her heart bumped, fear and joy tangled inside. She'd never been like this before either, and she wasn't quite sure what to do.

13

JEFF HAD LIVED THROUGH hell before, but it was never quite so—hellish. Sheldon was killing him. Running off, leaving him to search her out, and then, he'd find her off in a corner with a Yankee catcher, or a pitcher, or God forbid, both of them. The woman had been cursed with more sexual energy than a bunny rabbit.

He put the glass of ice water to his lips and drank deeply. He'd sworn off alcohol when thirty minutes into the night, she'd spiked his tonic water with Everclear. He considered looking for Sheldon again, but decided that he deserved a break, and if the woman were responsible for the destruction of his entire career in public relations, well, so be it. He'd hunt her down and make her pay later. Right now he needed to rest.

He collapsed onto an overstuffed couch, and watched the silver mermaid swimming in the champagne fountain. The woman went back and forth, hypnotizing him, until his sister arrived.

"Where's Sheldon?"

"Don't care," he answered.

"You're beaten."

"Yup, I'm a mere shell of the man I was when I arrived. Want some tonic water?"

She sank down next to him. "You're on the wagon? Things must be serious."

"Never more. In fact, when the clock strikes ten-thirty, I'm turning into a pumpkin," he said, closing his eyes and leaning his head back against the cushions.

"It's only ten, Jeff. Don't tell me you're ready to leave."

"I was ready to leave before I got here."

"Where's Andrew?"

He jerked his thumb towards the upstairs.

"What's he doing upstairs?"

Jeff opened one eye. "You really don't want to know."

"What?"

"Leave him alone, Mercy."

"I think I should have Jack and Honey sited in the men's room doing the deed. Just for old time's sake."

"Andrew's in love. Let him find his own misery."

"Love is a wonderful emotion, bringing fulfillment to all parties involved. Knowing your soul mate will be there for you every day for the rest of your life."

"One woman, the same woman, day after day for the rest of your life?" Jeff wiped his forehead. "Spoken like a female. Men need variety. Choice. Diversity. It's good for the country."

"Even a man in love? Like Andrew?"

Jeff waved a hand in the air. "Andrew's a lost cause. I'm speaking up for the rest of the male species."

She shot him a hopeless look. "Just as long as you don't get herpes."

A tired laugh escaped from him. "Thanks, Mom."

Mercedes closed her eyes. "Anytime, son."

JAMIE CHECKED HER WATCH and realized they'd been missing for thirty minutes. Hopefully, the cheerleader was keeping Arnie occupied.

After Andrew had made sure the coast was clear, she took a final tug on her skirt, and then crept outside. "Do you think anyone can tell?"

Andrew winked. "Not a soul. But me, of course. I'll live with the memory forever."

A mere two hours later, Andrew was escorting Jamie home in a cab. "I think the night was a huge success," she told him, kicking off her heels.

"Me, too," said Andrew, pulling her close against his side. "Your place or mine?"

"I'm thinking yours, tonight. Uptown. Money. Success. I think I can finally taste it."

He gave the cabbie instructions and then leaned down, meeting her in a deep kiss. "Let's explore that tasting thing in a little more detail."

IT WAS TWO O'CLOCK in the morning, and the combination of power, alcohol and sex had given Jamie a serious case of insomnia. Andrew was asleep, his head dark on the pillow, and Jamie went to the window and stared out on city lights that never dimmed.

He had told her that he loved her. *Loved her.* Not

liked. Not lusted. But loved. She pressed her cheek against the cold glass pane, trying to calm her over-heated body, her overheated mind, her overheated heart.

She'd stayed purposefully quiet because she had to think, and analyze, and figure out exactly what the hell she needed to do. He was so careful to never make demands on her time. She loved that he understood that; hell, his life was as bad as hers. Yet they managed fine.

Of course, she'd only known him two weeks. Could you fall in love in two weeks? She already knew the answer to that one. They might have only met two weeks ago, but she'd known him her entire life. A smile crossed her face because he was everything she was, and everything she wasn't. Surely that counted for something. And it wasn't like he'd be running off with his secretary anytime soon.

Best of all, the voices of doubt had stopped. She'd sprung the Newhouse deal. It was the Stanley Cup, the World Series and Dow 15,000, all with one simple yes. A moment of triumph when she knew she was just as good as Andrew. Maybe better. Okay, maybe not better, but still, just as good. She couldn't wait to send an e-mail to Walter telling him the news.

"I never pegged you for an exhibitionist." Two hands curved around her waist, and up to cover her breasts.

She leaned back against him, feeling his cock hard and insistent against her rear. "It's so quiet up here, like there's no one else alive."

His mouth sank into her shoulder, and then trailed down her back, and she took in a long breath of oxygen. His mouth moved lower, down the column of her spine, and the oxygen moved from her lungs.

He slipped in front of her, a shadow in the night. "There is no one else, Jamie. Just us. Tonight, there is no one else alive." And then his mouth moved lower, tasting the inside of her thigh. Her thighs fell apart, the muscles obeying the commands of her body. She was tired of fighting herself, she just wanted to give in. Let the world stand aside.

"I love you," she whispered softly, because she needed him to know.

His hands stroked her, and then he set his mouth on her. She gasped, unprepared for the dream-breaking pleasure of his tongue. His movements were sure and strong, as if he knew her own body better than she did. Slowly she rode the climax, no longer battling against it, because he had shattered her defenses finally and completely.

He picked her up in his arms and carried her to bed. This time they made love together, sharing the whispers and secrets of lovers, as if there was no one else alive.

Afterwards, she curled up in his arms, her head pillowed on his chest, and she listened to the steady beat of his heart.

It took ten beats of his heart before she feel asleep. Jamie McNamara no longer. Now she was merely Jamie, in love.

ONE WEEK FLEW BY, the days piling one on top of each other, but it was the nights she dreamed of. Every morning Jamie was in at seven-thirty, but each night she beat the vice presidents out the door. She'd turned from living in the office to professional clock watcher. But hey, she was a woman in love.

Their first night apart was supposed to be her trip to D.C. The general needed her back. Ah, it was good to be wanted.

The day of the trip dawned early, and she crawled out of bed at four a.m., dodging the nicely muscled male arm.

She planted a kiss on a sleepy shoulder, before heading out the door. "I'll be in around midnight," she said, and took out for La Guardia.

Of course, the weather had different ideas. The rain was pouring in buckets, the wind shaking the roof, and by mid-morning, she realized that her flight wasn't going anywhere.

Not that it mattered. Today was a travel day. Fully recognized hooky. She smiled to herself and took a cab back into the city. This was fate's way of telling her that today was the day. She would do some power shopping to find some lingerie. Something classy, dark and sexy. Maybe in silk…

She called Andrew's office, but he was having lunch with a client at the Four Seasons. Perfect. She whipped into Agent Provocateur and found a marvelous black teddy. Then she bought a single red rose, deciding to surprise him at the end of the lunch.

The lobby of the Four Seasons was bustling with the end of the lunch hour, and she found a seat near the bar, watching as the crowds filtered out. Every time a dark business suit filed past, her heart jumped, and she wondered if that would always be the case.

Eventually she saw the familiar dark head, and she waved discreetly.

He looked up, saw her, and stopped.

She stood, a broad smile on her face, until she saw his lunch companion.

Arnie Newhouse.

Her smile froze. However, never let it be said that Jamie McNamara didn't have discipline. She walked over and stuck out a hand—a cold hand—to Arnie.

"I hope you had a good lunch," she told him, the words coming automatically.

Arnie nodded once and then turned to Andrew. "Thanks," he said, then left, leaving the two of them alone.

A million conversations sped by in her brain, but she couldn't put the right words in order.

"I'm glad you're back," he said, kissing her on the cheek. It was awkward and stiff, and Andrew was not normally a cheek-kisser.

"I never went," she said. "The planes are grounded."

"Transportation seems to be your curse."

"Why are you having lunch with my client?"

"He wanted to get some financial advice. I knew how important he was to B&W. I thought I'd help out."

"Don't even try, Andrew. There are two possibilities and neither is pretty. Are you trying to steal my client?" She was praying that he said yes, because a conniving, backstabbing Andrew was preferable to the other alternative.

"You know me better than that."

Yes. Yes, she did. She knew him well, knew how much he took care of the people he loved. It was her blessing and her curse that Andrew Brooks, financial wunderkind, loved her.

"How did I get the Newhouse deal?"

He blew out a breath, his eyes nervous, chasing the horizon. Finally, his gaze made it back to her. "Don't make me do this, Jamie. Some things are better left under the table. Used chewing gum, for instance."

"Do you think this is funny?"

"No."

"How did I get the Newhouse deal?" she repeated, leaning back against the stone pillar behind her. She needed the support because right at this moment her legs didn't want to do it.

Andrew stuck his hands in his pockets, his change rattling. Finally he answered with the truth. "I told Arnie I'd give him financial advice gratis. He jumped."

"In return for him signing on with Bond-Worthington?"

He nodded. "It's business, Jamie. Nothing more."

Oh, that was so easy for him to say. "Yes, but it's not my business. That's the problem, Andrew."

"I wanted to help you. And he brought it up first," he told her.

She locked her knees together, because it was very important that she didn't fall. "And you didn't tell me."

"It didn't seem important."

"That's such bullshit," she said, louder than she intended. Heads turned. For once she didn't care.

"I wanted to help you. That's what you do with people you love. You shouldn't be mad. Let's leave. We'll talk it through." He took her arm, ready to lead her out the door, ready to take over her life, ready to take over her career. She shook off the arm.

"I think the situation's pretty clear, isn't it?"

"I was just trying to help, Jamie. You can't be this mad. You got what you wanted. You got the account."

"Because of you," she said through clenched teeth.

"Yes," he said, as if that was an everyday occurrence. And she knew that if they stayed together, it would be an everyday occurrence.

"I need some time to think," she said. Actually, she needed time to run because he didn't realize what their relationship would cost her. She'd spent her life being independent, successful, earning her way wherever she went. It was a source of pride for her. It was the McNamara way.

"You can't be serious," he said, eyes blinking in shock. "I did you a favor. And you're ready to walk away?"

"I don't work like that."

"Everybody works like that."

"You know me better than that. My work is all I have."

"You have me," he said, moving a step closer, trapping her against the pillar. "Don't I count?"

He didn't know how much he counted. He didn't know how easy it would be to just slip into his arms, bury her head on his shoulder, and float away. Andrew was a man used to arranging his own life and everyone else's, and it'd be so easy to let it go. No, Andrew would never know how easy it would be for her to release all her goals, all her dreams, her entire life, simply because she loved him.

Jamie unlocked the muscles in her legs, and slipped from under his arm. "I have to go," she said.

She walked away without looking back, because deep in the shadows of her steely heart, she knew she wasn't that strong.

14

HER DAYS TURNED into a dull routine. She was at the gym at five. At six she was showered and at the office. At seven forty-five, she left the office and headed home. It was the same grind Jamie had followed for years, but right now she needed it more than ever.

Andrew didn't call, didn't press her, and that only made her love him more. Which made her madder, which made her work even harder, and so the cycle continued.

She was pedaling wildly on the recumbent bike when Stephanie came in.

"Wow, I had thought you were dead. You know, you keep up that pace, and you will die of a stroke. Women are more likely to die from strokes, did you know that?"

"No," Jamie answered and pedaled faster.

"Where have you been?"

"Busy."

"You look fat."

Jamie stopped pedaling.

Stephanie looked as innocent as she could manage. "I was getting tired of one-word answers."

"Sorry. Bad week."

"Work?"

Jamie shook her head.

"Oh."

Stephanie didn't say anything else, just climbed on the elliptical and began to pedal. "I had a good week myself. Got asked out on three dates."

Jamie tried to smile. "That's good news."

"No, it's excellent news. There's Bob, the bartender, who is twenty-three, built like a stallion, and has these marvelous chiseled cheekbones."

"Built like a stallion? You've seen him in a stallionesque position?"

"You are such a nasty. He's got these big, muscular pecs, you know, just like a stallion."

"Uh-huh. And who's date number two?"

"Peter in banking."

"What does Peter look like?"

"I don't know. I met him online."

"Aren't you worried?"

"Nah, he doesn't have my picture either. If he's too ratty, I'll just pretend I never showed. I do it all the time."

"Stephanie!"

"I've been stood up by people who I knew were there. The world is a cruel place, Jamie."

"Don't start."

"So, you're just going to get all whiney, aren't you?"

"I don't whine."

"This is the boyfriend?"

"This is the boyfriend."

"Did he cheat?"

"No."

"Lie?"

"No."

"Kick a dog?"

"No."

"Mistreat an animal in any way, shape or form?"

When confronted with the cold, hard logic in Stephanie's viewpoint, Andrew didn't seem awful at all. "He cooked up a deal so I could get a client."

"Oh… Sounds like heart-ripping betrayal to me." Then she whacked Jamie in the arm. "Are you for real? Do you realize how many women would give their size ten bodies to be in your shoes? Do you know how much I have to hate you at this moment?"

"I'm sorry, Steph."

"That's all right. The hate's passed. Let me explain the facts of life to you, Jamie. Does he love you?"

"Yes."

"Do you love him?"

"Yes."

"That's it, then. That's the entire book on life summed up in two questions. Don't be stupid, Jamie."

"I'm not stupid. I'm very smart."

Steph shot her an "I don't think so" look.

Jamie stopped pedaling because there was no one in the world that would ever understand her. Possibly because no one knew that when you went to four different high schools in four years, you learned that friendships and relationships weren't made to last.

Achievements lasted. A career lasted. So how could she stay with a man who made her own achievements look like a first-year rookie's? "I'm insanely jealous of him."

"Why? He has bigger boobs than you?"

"He's smarter, more successful, and works harder than I do. Sometimes I look at him and wonder how I can compete with that."

"Oh." Stephanie pulled up the Pilates ball and balanced on it like a chair. "That's not so easy. I had a guy who I was over the moon for, but he was a total hottie, and I was, uh, not."

"What happened?"

"We broke up."

"I thought you were supposed to make me feel better."

"Excuse me, you have a boyfriend, a size six body and a successful career. If anyone needs sympathy here, it's me."

"I don't know if I have a boyfriend. And you have three dates."

Stephanie grinned. "You're right. I feel better already. If you weren't sweaty, I'd hug you."

"My piss-poor self-esteem thanks you for that life affirmation."

Oh to hell with it all. Jamie jumped off and caught her in a hug. It was an awkward moment because Jamie had never been a hugger, but she hadn't had many friends, either, and she thought she'd found a good one. "We have to find you a boyfriend, too. Maybe one of the three will turn out to be Mr. Right."

"So you're keeping yours?"

"Sometimes it hurts when I'm with him."

"I've heard that about love."

"I don't want it to hurt."

"Welcome to the real world."

EVERY DAY ANDREW CHECKED his answering machine. He knew if Jamie would call, she'd just call his cell, but his cell was quiet, except for the work calls. So every day he'd come home to his empty apartment and check the answering machine. Just in case.

He wanted to call her, wanted to send her a dozen roses, but that wasn't the way to win Jamie. She was thoughtful, methodical, and would perform a thorough risk analysis on their relationship.

He'd flown out to L.A. three times, and God knows, he hated the cross-country flights, but he hated an empty apartment more. She'd left her toothbrush there and one red shoe. He thought she'd at least call to get her shoe back, but she didn't.

On Thursday he had come home and found the light on his answering machine blinking. He jammed the button, waiting to hear her voice. Sadly, it was his brother's.

"Drew, when are you going to be home? George let me up—"

Andrew turned around, and found his brother was sprawled in the chair, one shot glass tipped over in front of him. "Does my apartment look like Grand Central?"

Jeff squinted. "Nope."

"Why are you here?"

"She wants to move in with me. She said that she'd arrange a wardrobe malfunction at a Knicks game unless I agreed."

"At a basketball game?"

"She's heartless. A barracuda." Jeff buried his face in his hands. "She said that I slept with her."

"You don't remember?"

Jeff merely whimpered in agreement.

"Was this before or after you started drinking?"

"I don't know. It's all a blur. She's not going to leave me alone now. Once they get a taste of the magic, they don't let go."

"I don't want to hear this. I have my own problems to worry about."

"Rich people don't have problems."

Money solved a lot of problems. It kept a roof over his head, fed his family, and he was able to afford a taxi when it rained, but it didn't solve everything. It didn't bring Jamie back. He rubbed against his heart with a fist.

Andrew cast a long, hard look at the bottle of whiskey on the table. "Does it help?"

"Only when I think about it."

That did it. Andrew fell into the opposite chair, poured a shot, and then drank. The gold liquid ran down his throat and he waited for the numbing to begin. It didn't, so he poured another one. After five shots, he still wasn't numb, but now he was glad for the company. "Jamie's gone."

Jeff looked up. "You lost her?"

"I don't know."

Jeff shook his head. "How can you not know?"

"I don't know. She's thinking."

"Thinking? Bad. You're so screwed, man. What'd you do?"

"Nothing."

Jeff snickered. "You couldn't do nothing if they tied up all four hands and strung you up. What'd you do?"

"I ran some interference. Pulled some strings."

"Strings?" Jeff pointed at him. "You have to stop with the strings. Women hate that."

Andrew rubbed his face. "I can't."

"Dude, you have to stop. Just…do it."

"Somebody has to take care of things."

"You just have to meddle."

"Do not."

"Do, too."

"Not," said Andrew. But it was his curse. It'd taken two hours and a bottle of his best Scotch to convince Boone Slager that Stella in 43C wasn't a prostitute. In the end he had told Boone that she was an agoraphobic and slightly eccentric, with an odd desire to teach knitting. And of course, she didn't like strangers to talk about it, so if Boone could keep quiet, Andrew would appreciate it.

He'd almost ruined Stella's life, and now, without Jamie, he worried that he ruined his own. Since he was fourteen, Andrew hadn't bothered to ask permission from anyone, he'd mainly gone ahead and taken care of whatever problems that needed to be fixed. No one had ever complained before. In fact, most people considered it one of his best traits. And now he was supposed to change it?

"I need another drink," muttered Jeff, not really helping with Andrew's psychological evaluation. Probably a good thing.

"Why aren't women easy?"

Jeff sniffed in the air. "I read that on a T-shirt."

"Do you think she'll come back?"

"If she loves you, she will."

"What if she doesn't?"

Jeff never answered, he had fallen asleep.

Bears are running at the corner of Broad and Wall. Bull Market Jack's run of luck has ended, and the Hummer Honey has left the building. Sources close to Jack say the poor man is heartbroken. Here at the Choo, we hope that Honey will return, because Jack without Honey is no fun at all.

JAMIE PICKED UP her eight ball and read the message.

Someone is thinking of you.

Yeah, that made two of them. Every day she'd looked at the phone, wanting to call, wanting to tell him that she loved him. But she didn't. She was a McNamara, and McNamara's were disciplined, driven…

Dejected.

Helen came into her office and handed her the pink message slip.

"A message. Andrew Brooks."

Oh, God. "He called the main line?"

"Wants a meeting to discuss housing indicators."

"Andrew Brooks?" Walter poked his head in the office. "That's the major leagues, Jamie, my girl. But don't let him sweet-talk you into joining Shearson, Brooks, Panhower and Bloom."

"It's nothing, sir."

He shook a finger at her. "It's never nothing, kiddo."

HE MET HER AT CAPPY'S. She was nervous, scared, and for a very risk-averse person, seeing Andrew again was a risk. A huge risk. A life-altering risk. But in the end, she didn't have a choice.

"Thanks for meeting me," he told her, his eyes searching hers.

"Yeah," she muttered, keeping her gaze determinedly down.

"I wanted to tell you something. When I was twenty-three, I met Charlie O'Donnell, the vice president of B of A at a charity golf game for the March of Dimes. I was a nobody, but I had bribed the organizer to assign me to a power-foursome. When Charlie hit his ball into the trees, I told him that my eyes were bad, and I couldn't tell where it hit. I lied, he knew I lied, and he saved three strokes against his boss. Was it wrong for me to do that?"

She looked up, met his eyes square on. "Probably."

"But then he hired Mercedes for a summer internship at his mag; she needed a job because her landlord was raising her rent, and her roommate had gone off to USC. It was either that or she'd have to move back in with Mom, who was living at the time in a studio apartment. Still think it was wrong?"

"Yes."

"You're a hard woman, Jamie McNamara."

She blinked at the feeling in his eyes. How could anyone deny that? "That's why you love me."

"Do you love me?"

Jamie licked her lips before answering, her nerves eating a hole in her gut. "Yes."

"Then why the obstacles?"

"You're a man."

"What does that have to do with anything?"

"For men, the world revolves around bacon under the table, information garnered over a golf game or in a barbershop, and deals consummated under the influence of alcohol or sex. I don't play by those rules, Andrew. I don't cut corners."

"Life isn't fair, Jamie. If you play by the rules, you're always competing against someone who won't. I'm not talking about breaking the law here, I'm just talking about using whatever advantage you can to get ahead."

"I don't cheat."

"Letting someone help you isn't cheating."

"Andrew, you're trying to justify things that you know you can't justify."

"Fine. Do you think I'm unethical?"

"No."

"You can live with the things I do in business?"

Jamie nodded.

"Then why aren't we together?"

"Because I…" she trailed off.

"Because you what?"

"I'm not as good as you are."

"You could be. Did you know that? You could be better than me, Jamie. You've got a sharp eye for people's soft spots and you're much better at knowing how to use it. I just analyze data. You notice life."

"Really?"

"I want to help you succeed, Jamie, not because you need it, but because I love you. To make it in business, you have to accept favors, you have to help people, and people will help you. Sometimes it does take a village. I want to be your village. I want to be your country. I want to be your world. Because you're my world, Jamie."

There he sat, simply staring at her like she was his world. She bit her lip, fighting to keep control. God, she was losing it.

He took her hand, put their two hands together, palm to palm. "I used to think that everyone else was in on some punchline that I never understood. Jeff, Mercedes, even Mom, they always were happy. But I couldn't be happy. And then I met you, and I realized you were as miserable at life as I was. And then a miracle happened. The first day you woke up in my bed, I noticed the clouds hanging low over the park. When we walked down here on our first date, did you notice the smell of roasted hazelnuts rising above the exhaust fumes? I did. I never had stopped and smelled the roses before, hell, I never even noticed the roses before, and it's not like I'm going on sunlit walks on the beach, but I don't need to. You're my world, you're my beach, you're my rose. You're all I need to be happy. No one else understands this drive inside me like you do."

She bit her lip because he was going to make her cry, and she didn't want to cry. Tears were a sign of weakness. Eventually she was ready to speak, he could use all his pretty words, but the truth would never change. "But how do I lay down next to you knowing that your deal is bigger than mine, your profile is going to be in *Forbes,* and I never will? I'll be a peroxide blonde with an alcohol problem, and the next thing you know, I'll be getting Botox injections, which I suppose is better than being fifty and being single, with only my cat for company, but not by much."

"There's only one solution."

"What?"

"I don't know if I should tell you. You might think I'm trying to help you again."

"Tell me."

"You won't be mad at me?"

"Only if you don't tell me."

"All right. Don't compete against me. Join me."

Jamie shook a finger in his direction. "Oh yeah, I can see how that would go over. The partners looking in my direction: 'Sleeping with the boss, McNamara?'"

"I wasn't talking about Shearson, Brooks, Panhower and Bloom. We'll start our own fund. Brooks and McNamara. Partners. I know a guy, hell, I know a million guys, and I have the backing. It'll be a walk in the park."

"Go into business together?"

"Yeah. Next time I'm on the cover of *Forbes,* I want you with me. As an equal partner."

"Except that I'd just cruise by on your laurels."

"Oh, no, the sleeping with the boss excuse won't cut it with me. You're going to have laurels all your own, so then I can retire early. Maybe take up woodworking."

"You really mean this?"

"I never say anything I don't mean, Jamie. You should have figured that out by now."

"You're not just saying it?"

"Do you still not get it? That's why I love you because you're going to have laurels of your own. You work harder than anyone else and your brain never stops clicking. In fact, I fully expect you to lift yourself off me some morning and say, 'Steel. And the petrochemical industry. It's the way to save the rust belt!'"

"Steel?"

"If I'm in the middle of sex, and it's my story, it's going to be steel." Then his eyes got serious and he reached across the table, taking her hand. "Don't walk away, Jamie. I know it won't be easy, I know I'm not the world's most sensitive guy, but I'll do my best. You're my world, my rose, my heart, please don't leave me alone again."

"You're going to make me cry," she said, because the tears were already welling up in her eyes.

"Is that a yes?"

Jamie nodded once.

"Yes!" he yelled and then walked around the table. He had to kiss her, it had been too long, and the world was a gray place without her.

Slowly a sound emerged from the fog. Applause. He pulled back and looked around the room. Okay, so maybe they were going to make the papers tomorrow, but he really didn't care. Not anymore.

"She said yes," he told the world. And then he began to kiss her again.

* * * * *

Don't miss the next installment of
THE RED CHOO DIARIES!
Jeff's sexy romance, BEYOND DARING,
is available March 2007 from Harlequin Blaze.
Turn the page for a sneak peek.

1

THERE HE WAS, completely comfortable in the kitchen, chef's knife in hand. It was criminal that a man could be so tasty, so buff, so studly, and yet still work in the stab-you-in-the-back world of PR.

Sheldon Summerville pulled at the tank top and leaned back against the wall, adapting her patented vacant, yet still sexy stare. As soon as he felt the weight of her stare, he looked up, took a long eye-drinking of her skin, and then went back to chopping peppers.

"Can you put some clothes on?"

Even the voice was sexy. Her nipples hardened under the thin material, without cold air, artificial device, and/or a drenching of water. Her mouth opened to snarl at him, but it would ruin her image, so instead she walked to the kitchen, leaned one hip against the edge of the granite counter, and let the long cascade of her hair fall over one breast.

"You're complaining?"

His strong, capable hands never stopped in the mechanical chopping motion. She'd had dreams of those hands on her.

"Not complaining, just trying to be helpful." He smiled at her, a teethy advertising smile, possibly attributed to Toothbrite toothpaste. She suspected that he knew she hated it—both the toothpaste and the smile—which was why he did it.

"Is there something I can do?" she purred, her eyes gleaming when his hand stopped for a small second.

He shook his hand and continued working. "Hangover this morning?"

She used one hand to lift her hair in a ponytail, making sure her breasts were pushed out a size larger than her normal B-cup. His gaze drifted.

Her lips curved upward.

"Are you ever closed for business?" he asked.

Her eyes, normally vacuous and sultry, looked down meekly so that he wouldn't see the rage. Rage implied a depth that she didn't want to possess.

She backed away from the kitchen, the knife, the man with the strong, capable hands, and padded barefoot across the room.

"I think I'll take a shower," she said, and then slipped the tank over her head. He didn't even look up, so she slid the signature red panties down over her legs. "You don't mind, do you?" she asked, her heart rapping inside her.

He looked up, his dark gaze lit over her, and she felt each and every touch. This time he didn't smile, just lowered his head and continued the whap-whap-whap against the cutting board.

Dismissed.

She left her clothes in a sordid heap in the middle of the floor, and retreated to the loneliness of his shower. She turned on the warm spray and let it wash over her body, slipping between her breasts and thighs. She shouldn't have been alone. He should be there, too. Life truly wasn't fair. Men in the media weren't supposed to have scruples. She was sure of it.

JEFF CONTINUED CHOPPING until all eleven green peppers had been chopped into precise, green triangles. When there were no more peppers left to chop, he exhaled slowly, wiping the sweat from his forehead. It was a good thing she'd never touched him because he wasn't sure he could have stopped himself from pouncing.

He clicked on the television, letting the perky morning news shows dull the throbbing ache of his erection. Damn.

Last night had been a stupid idea, but every night with Sheldon was a stupid idea. She had conveniently told his secretary she was going to the notorious club Crobar. Jeff, knowing that would mean multiple doses of alcoholic beverages, had shown up at ten, hoping to play responsible chaperone. At 10:09, he'd pulled her off the bartender, at 10:13, he'd pulled her off the New York Ranger's goalie, and when he caught her kissing the bouncer, he knew it was past time for her to go home.

They'd argued until the cops came, threatening to arrest her, which would be exactly what she wanted. So Jeff had poured her into a taxi and taken her home. With him. It seemed like a good idea at the time. It still seemed like a good idea six hours later when he woke up in his bed alone, finding her still snoozing happily in the guest bedroom. In fact, he had congratulated himself on finally lassoing Sheldon into some sort of obedient servitude.

However, just now he had stopped congratulating himself because his penis had grown an extra fourteen inches, demanding to be inserted into the golden skin that rested beneath her thighs. Brazilian. Why Brazilian?

He groaned, loud, ragged. A rutting stag deprived of dinner. Would she notice if he spent the next thirty minutes jerking off? Probably. She'd want to help. That was her way.

He threw the peppers, all eleven of them into the sauté pan and cranked up the burner, watching the thick skins pulse as the heat licked them into submission. He took eight eggs from the SubZero and kicked the door shut with extra force. It didn't help ease the pain, but these were desperate times.

One by one he cracked the eggs, stirring them into a fine glop of something that resembled the aftermath of particularly athletic sex, and then poured them over the tenderized green peppers.

Life really wasn't fair. He didn't want to want Sheldon. She was off-limits, with a capital *O,* little *f,* little *f.* O-F-F. F-F-O. He recited the little jingle in his head, while his dick still demanded to be reacquainted with her nethers. *Reacquainted.* Oh, that was good. Did it count if he couldn't remember the original acquainting? Probably. Sex was sex, whether your memory cooperated or not.

Expertly he flipped the omelet, shredding some gouda over the smooth, yellow body of the eggs.

Eventually, the cheese melted, sliding into each and every crevice of the sensual delicacy. Jeff flipped it onto a plate, ruthlessly sliced it into two halves, and then laid the plates on the bar.

When exposed to the sunlight, it looked liked nothing more than breakfast. His mind latched onto the commonplace thoughts, pushing aside visions of naked thighs, breasts, all being caressed by the warm waters of his shower. Damn it. He could hear the water running, so he thought he was safe. Thought she'd given him a reprieve.

He was wrong.

Sheldon came into the living room, using a towel to dry the long hair. The rest of her was still dripping wet. Nude, and dripping wet. His eyes noticed, his hands began to shake, and his cock…well, he really didn't want to think about the tortured appendage that used to be functional at the moment.

She walked, walked being a very inadequate word to describe the movement of her body, over to the small pile of underwear, picking up her bra and panties.

"Can't believe I was such a slob," she said, her eyes catching at the waistband of his boxers. "My, my, my…" she said, clicking her tongue against her teeth. He hated the victory in her eyes, but he was a weakened piece of flesh. It was self-preservation that kept him motionless.

Her hand reached toward him, and he closed his eyes, steeling himself for her touch. He was strong. He was invincible. And mostly, there were ten million reasons that he could not touch her. Again.

"An omelet? You are talented," she whispered, her hand flirting near his waist. Yet still she didn't touch him.

He swallowed.

She noticed.

Then, her hand fell away, and he told himself that he was relieved, lying bastard that he was. But then, the gates of hell opened before him. She leaned down and touched the tip of her tongue to the engorged, pained, tortured, yet still panting-like-a-happy-puppy, tip of his cock.

She popped back up, wearing a smile of victory and nothing else. Then she wiggled her brows at him and strolled back into the bathroom. He couldn't suppress his groan.

"I heard that," she yelled.

At the moment he didn't care.

Happily ever after is just the beginning...

Turn the page for a sneak preview of
DANCING ON SUNDAY AFTERNOONS
by
Linda Cardillo

Harlequin Everlasting—Every great love
has a story to tell. ™
A brand-new line from Harlequin Books
launching this February!

Prologue

Giulia D'Orazio
1983

I had two husbands—Paolo and Salvatore.

Salvatore and I were married for thirty-two years. I still live in the house he bought for us; I still sleep in our bed. All around me are the signs of our life together. My bedroom window looks out over the garden he planted. In the middle of the city, he coaxed tomatoes, peppers, zucchini—even grapes for his wine—out of the ground. On weekends, he used to drive up to his cousin's farm in Waterbury and bring back manure. In the winter, he wrapped the peach tree and the fig tree with rags and black rubber hoses against the cold, his massive, coarse hands gentling those trees as if they were his fragile-skinned babies. My neighbor, Dominic Grazza, does that for me now. My boys have no time for the garden.

In the front of the house, Salvatore planted roses. The roses I take care of myself. They are giant, cream-colored, fragrant. In the afternoons, I like to sit out on the porch with my coffee, protected from the eyes of the neighborhood by that curtain of flowers.

Salvatore died in this house thirty-five years ago. In the last months, he lay on the sofa in the parlor so he could be in the middle of everything. Except for the two oldest boys, all the children were still at home and we ate together every evening. Salvatore could see the dining room table from the sofa, and he could hear everything that was said. "I'm not dead, yet," he told me. "I want to know what's going on."

When my first grandchild, Cara, was born, we brought her to him, and he held her on his chest, stroking her tiny head. Sometimes they fell asleep together.

Over on the radiator cover in the corner of the parlor is the portrait Salvatore and I had taken on our twenty-fifth anniversary. This brooch I'm wearing today, with the diamonds—I'm wearing it in the photograph also—Salvatore gave it to me that day. Upstairs on my dresser is a jewelry box filled with necklaces and bracelets and earrings. All from Salvatore.

I am surrounded by the things Salvatore gave me, or did for me. But, God forgive me, as I lie alone now in my bed, it is Paolo I remember.

Paolo left me nothing. Nothing, that is, that my

family, especially my sisters, thought had any value. No house. No diamonds. Not even a photograph.

But after he was gone, and I could catch my breath from the pain, I knew that I still had something. In the middle of the night, I sat alone and held them in my hands, reading the words over and over until I heard his voice in my head. I had Paolo's letters.

* * * * *

Be sure to look for
DANCING ON SUNDAY AFTERNOONS
available January 30, 2007.
And look, too, for our other
Everlasting title available,
FALL FROM GRACE by Kristi Gold.

FALL FROM GRACE is a deeply emotional story
of what a long-term love really means.
As Jack and Anne Morgan discover,
marriage vows can be broken—
but they can be mended, too.
And the memories of their marriage have
an unexpected power to bring back a love
that never really left....

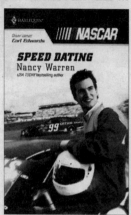

HARLEQUIN *Romance*®

What a month!

In February watch for

Rancher and Protector
Part of the Western Weddings miniseries
BY JUDY CHRISTENBERRY

The Boss's Pregnancy Proposal
BY RAYE MORGAN

Also in February, expect
MORE of what you love
as the Harlequin Romance line
increases to six titles per month.

Silhouette Desire

Don't miss the first book
in THE ROYALS trilogy:

THE FORBIDDEN PRINCESS
(SD #1780)

by national bestselling author

DAY LECLAIRE

Moments before her loveless royal wedding,
Princess Alyssa was kidnapped by a mysterious man
who'd do anything to stop the ceremony. Even if that
meant marrying the forbidden princess himself!

On sale February 2007 from Silhouette Desire!

THE ROYALS
Stories of scandals and secrets
amidst the most powerful palaces.

Make sure to read the other titles in the series:
THE PRINCE'S MISTRESS
On sale March 2007
THE ROYAL WEDDING NIGHT
On sale April 2007

*Available wherever books are sold, including most
bookstores, supermarkets, discount stores and drugstores.*

Visit Silhouette Books at www.eHarlequin.com SDTFP0207

REQUEST YOUR FREE BOOKS!

2 FREE NOVELS PLUS 2 FREE GIFTS!

HARLEQUIN®

Blaze®

Red-hot reads!

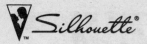

HARLEQUIN®

Blaze™

COMING NEXT MONTH

#303 JINXED! Jacquie D'Alessandro, Jill Shalvis, Crystal Green
Valentine Anthology
Valentine's Day. If she's lucky, a girl can expect to receive dark chocolate, red roses and fantastic sex! If she's not…well, she can wind up with a Valentine's Day curse…and fantastic sex! Join three of Harlequin Blaze's bestselling authors as they show how three very unlucky women can end up getting *very* lucky….

#304 HITTING THE MARK Jill Monroe
Danielle Ford has been a successful con artist most of her life. Giving up the habit has been hard, but she's kicked it. Until Eric Reynolds, security chief at a large Reno casino, antes up a challenge she can't back away from—one that touches her past and ups her odds on bedding sexy Eric.

#305 DON'T LOOK BACK Joanne Rock
Night Eyes, Bk. 1
Hitting the sheets with P.I. Sean Beringer might have been a mistake. While the sex is as hot as the man, NYPD detective Donata Casale is struggling to focus on their case. They need to wrap up this investigation fast. Then she'll be free to fully indulge in this fling.

#306 AT HER BECK AND CALL Dawn Atkins
Doing It…Better!, Bk. 2
Autumn Beskin can bring a man to his knees. The steamy glances from her new boss, Mike Fields, say she hasn't lost her touch. But while he may be interested in more than her job performance, he hasn't made a move. Guess she'll have to nudge this fling along.

#307 HOT MOVES Kristin Hardy
Sex & the Supper Club II, Bk. 2
Professional dancer Thea Mitchell knows all the right steps—new job, new city, new life. But then Brady McMillan joins her Latin tango dance class and suddenly she's got two left feet. When he makes his move, with naughty suggestions and even naughtier kisses, she doesn't know what to expect next!

#308 PRIVATE CONFESSIONS Lori Borrill
What does a woman do when she discovers that her secret online sex partner is actually her real-life boss—the man she's been lusting after for two years? She goes for it! Trisha Bain isn't sure how to approach Logan Moore with the knowledge that he's Pisces47, only that she wants to make the fantasy a reality. Fast…

www.eHarlequin.com

HBCNM0107